Embrace the Night

Veil of Shadows
Book Eight

M. R. Pritchard

Paperback ISBN: 9781957709482

About Embrace the Night

Haunted by Shadows, Bound by Fate

As Jed and Shay embark on their journey to California, the path ahead is fraught with peril. Angels, hell-bent on Jed's demise, and Demons coveting Shay for their own sinister purposes, shadow their every step.

All seems to be progressing smoothly until a heartbroken ghost intervenes, diverting their course and leading to Shay's abduction. With each twist in the road, danger emerges anew, compelling Jed to contemplate the solitary and perilous route to ruin.

In a relentless pursuit against supernatural forces and unforeseen threats, Jed must navigate a treacherous landscape where allies are scarce, and the odds of survival grow slimmer.

Will he defy the odds to rescue Shay, or will the Demons of their journey propel him toward a desolate path of self-destruction? The road to California unfolds as a haunting odyssey, where every turn unearths not only the perils of the present but also the ghosts of Jed's past.

CHAPTER 1

SHAY WASN'T ONE TO BELIEVE IN GHOSTS BUT SHE couldn't shake the feeling that someone was watching her.

Gooseflesh rose on her arms and the back of her neck, and it wasn't from the water she was washing in. Jed wasn't far away–he rarely was–but Shay took some time for privacy by the cold mountain stream. She didn't want to call out to him like a fearful child. From her periphery she momentarily saw a wavering figure in white, and then it was gone. She told herself it was nothing then turned and found Nero stepping onto the riverbank.

"Hey, boy," Shay wrapped herself in a blanket and walked toward the black stallion. "It's been a while." Shay stroked Nero's face.

They hadn't seen Nero since the last night they'd spent in Montana while Jed healed enough to travel. That had been several days ago. Jed and Shay had traveled through most of

Idaho, sticking close to the National Forests where rest stops and stores were present but the population wasn't. They'd driven past Boise National Forest at midnight and avoided most of the dead wandering out of the towns and cities. Jed had been correct; the dead were headed west, toward California. They'd seen them moving in herds like a cattle drive without a cowboy. The largest of the zombie horde wasn't far from Fort Bragg. Jed had a plan to travel south to avoid them, intercepting Sparrow before it got too dangerous.

Jed and Shay were making their way through a portion of Oregon that was mostly uninhabited; there wasn't much to see besides foothills and the prairies and the mountains in the distance. It was scenic at least. The backdrop to their travels didn't force one to dwell on the fact that the dead were walking and biting.

Shay was surprised she didn't see Nero as they drove. She figured that he'd found some other route, maybe one with wild horses so he wasn't lonely. It's all Shay could hope for her beloved friend.

"I miss you," Shay said as she stroked Nero's flank and noticed how shiny his coat had become now that he was living free. She hoped he'd found happiness in the fresh air and open fields and had recovered from what they'd endured at the ranch in Montana.

Nero huffed and rubbed his head against her shoulder before drinking from the stream.

Shay dressed in clean clothes then gathered her belongings. She paused, finding a small ring with a blue stone tucked between the rocks at the bank of the stream. These days, money was no good most places but a ring could be a wager. Shay tucked it in her pocket, then went to find Jed.

"Don't be a stranger," she told Nero with the wave of her hand.

Chapter 2

Clyburn followed the fading scent of Shay across the Montana foothills. He didn't care to hide his hideous form of a man running on all fours, elbows and knees bent at awkward angles. His claws tapped on the crumbling asphalt of the road. He leapt over broken down cars, agile as a panther. Being a Crossroads Demon, Clyburn was nothing more than a shadow in the periphery to a human on the Earthen plane. One moment he was there, the next he was a figment of their imagination; an errant shadow of a bird flying overhead, the whisper of a heavy tree branch in the wind. Nothing, apparently. Clyburn moved swiftly with ease through the Earthen plane, undisturbed since the balance was off. The Veil separating the realms was thinner than ever now that a Hellion walked the Earthen plane.

Clyburn stopped in the road, sniffed the pile of ashes that were once a punishing Angel. There was a drop of Shay's blood. Clyburn licked it off the asphalt, tilted his nose to the sky and sniffed. She'd backtracked. Clyburn went off running and fueled by the drop of Shay's blood, he ran faster.

Stopping at a fork in the road, Clyburn smelled Shay in both directions. Humans were creatures of habit. And Shay-baby knew where she belonged: on the ranch. Clyburn figured she changed her mind, left that abomination Jed and went home.

He wanted her. He wanted the shiny dangle of the Cross-roads Demon ring and bracelet. The old gold was ancient, powerful, his. He'd kill Jed for taking it. He'd kill Jed for taking Shay.

"Precious," Clyburn grumbled as he missed the feel of it on his wrist even though he'd never touched it before ascending. Jed had cut it off the previous Demon and ran off with it. It belonged on Clyburn's hand. It was *his*.

He leapt over fallen trees two at a time and veered into the forests of the foothills to hide his shadow from the sunlight that broke the cloud cover. He slid under the chain that crossed a hidden driveway and slowed his pace.

Clyburn prowled, hunted. He stuck to the shadows as he walked down the driveway. He wanted to surprise them, shock them; he wanted to consume them. The crossbreed abomination would be first. Clyburn licked his lips, imagining the taste of sweet meat, imagining the crunch of magic-filled bones. Yes, he would eat Jed first. But Shay, she would be a treat to be savored. She would display nicely at his hovel in Hell. He thought about the chains he could lock her in, the table he could strap her to. His filthy body hardened at thoughts of Shay at his mercy. He'd had thoughts of her like that since the moment he met her at that dive bar near Colstrip. She was easy, innocent, and followed his lead that night. Then she played hard to get. Clyburn knew better. He knew she craved his hard body just as he craved her softness. He'd make her see. He'd show her. Shay was his.

Clyburn stopped, dropped low to the ground, and watched the clearing ahead of him. There was a shack but nothing more. Fresh tire tracks in the dirt driveway led Clyburn to believe that they had been there. He walked closer, unafraid. Her scent was strong and it led him to a tree near a bubbling stream. Strips of cloth hung from a branch. Clyburn ripped them down and smelled them. Jed's scent was strong but Shay's was there. He examined the stream and tire tracks under the tree. They'd been there then left.

Clyburn cursed himself for assuming she'd gone home. He took the wrong path where the road bisected. She wasn't going home, she was still leaving.

Clyburn snarled and roared. He dug his claws into the dirt, using purchase in the soil as a launching pad and took off.

CHAPTER 3

"Do you believe in ghosts?" Shay asked Jed as he drove a winding, empty road.

Jed gave her a hard look. "Ghosts are rarely ghosts." He bit the inside of his cheek, preparing himself for what she was about to say. He'd warned her to tell him when she saw something strange. She was new to his world. Things that'd seemed normal rarely were. They held a deeper meaning, sometimes a darker meaning or message that something was coming.

"What did you see?" he asked.

Shay thumbed behind them. "Back at that stream I thought I saw a white figure. But then Nero was there."

"Did it say anything?" Jed asked.

"Not that I heard."

"How long did you see it for?"

"Just a second. I think." Shay rubbed her arms, remembering the feeling of being watched as she bathed.

Jed tapped his fingers on the steering wheel and chose his next words carefully. He didn't want to scare Shay. She'd probably punch him in the throat if he ever appeared threatening. He still had thoughts of her stabbing that Angel in the chest and killing him. Jed never wanted her to turn that wrath on him. He took a cleansing breath and slowed the Jeep so he could look at her.

"One second is enough to bring death to us both." Jed touched her hand. "If it happens again, I need to know right then."

Shay nodded, feeling like an idiot. She reminded herself that the world was different now. Nothing would be the same. She didn't want to be making mistakes like that night with Clyburn. Shay swallowed hard. She'd never get over that guilt.

"It's okay."

"This is all new to me." Shay touched the tattoos on Jed's wrist with her free hand. "Childlike fears and weird feelings; I've learned to ignore them."

"That is the way of the Earthen plane." He rubbed her hand, soothing her. He knew he needed to stop because touching her too much brought thoughts of other things, other needs and desires that he would not burden Shay with right now. She needed time to heal and learn. She needed time to accept her new reality or change her mind. Jed didn't want to let her go, but a life with him would be dangerous and he'd warned her. She could change her mind at any time, Jed reminded himself daily.

"Tell me about Nero," Jed said as he accelerated the Jeep again. "I didn't see him while we were parked."

Shay smiled, and Jed didn't miss the way her eyes lit up at seeing her horse again. "He was just there, drinking from the stream. Completely surprised me. He must be learning stealth moves from those wild horses."

Jed read the road sign for California as they passed Silver Lake. He turned onto Route 97 and drove south.

Jed didn't pretend to be an expert on horses or how they snuck up on people, but he hoped Shay would see Nero again since it brought her happiness. After all that had happened, that was all he could wish for her.

"Oh look." Shay pointed to a sign. "There's a diner nearby." She patted her stomach. "I could really go for some greasy diner food. We could stop and see if they have French toast."

"No." Jed shook his head.

"Why not?"

"I'm never eating French toast again."

"Why?" Shay asked.

"I want nothing tethered to the memory of French toast besides that first moment I saw you."

"Well, ain't that the sweetest thing a guy has ever said to me?" Shay rested her chin on her hand and batted her eyes at him exaggeratedly. "To forever taint a man's desire for French toast. I never thought I had it in me."

Jed laughed.

Shay pointed toward the tree line. "There she is."

Jed looked. One second there was a woman in a white dress, staring. The next second she was gone.

"Is that what you saw by the river?" Jed asked.

"Yeah. That's her. Weird that it's twice now."

The sign for the diner came again.

Jed decided he could go for some greasy diner food as well. He really wanted a bottomless mug of hot coffee.

"Look," Shay pointed to the window, "they still have electricity and there's people here."

Jed turned in to the parking lot of the diner, parked the Jeep and turned off the ignition.

"Yes. I hope they have grilled cheese." Shay was tucking her bugout bag behind the passenger seat.

"If anything is sketchy, we are out," Jed warned. "I mean *anything*."

The diner was running like normal. The dead hadn't ruined this area, yet. Jed wondered if he should warn them that the horde was coming, probably by next week, and they should prepare to get out.

"Tell me if you see that woman in white again. I don't care if you're in the bathroom, Shay. It's more than a coincidence." Jed flipped through his spell book and racked his brain for anything he'd read in the Peabody Library all those years ago that might apply to the woman Shay had seen twice now.

"I'll tell ya," Shay promised as she got out of the Jeep and closed the door.

Jed held the diner door open for Shay and they were

greeted by a smiling waitress snapping gum. "Just you all?" she asked.

"Two," Shay said.

"I got a window seat over here for you." The waitress led them to a window booth. Jed would have preferred the corner booth where he could get a better view of the room and not have people at his back, but he tried to tell himself to relax. This wasn't the Lame Deer Casino. He didn't smell death seeping from the walls. Jed took a laminated menu from the waitress.

"Can I get you both drinks?"

Jed motioned to Shay.

"I'll have a diet coke," Shay said.

"Coffee and a water, please." Jed touched the napkin that was wrapped around the silverware.

Shay noticed he was looking for something and leaned closer to him. "I think we're safe here. This doesn't look like a place that would house Angels or Demons."

"You'd be surprised," Jed said with a half-raise of the corner of his mouth.

The waitress brought their drinks and took their orders. Shay got the grilled cheese with fries. Jed ordered a cheeseburger with chips.

"If you want, we have a motel out back. Hot water and soft beds." The waitress looked at Shay. "The little things that help us feel human."

Shay turned to Jed. "A hot shower sounds nice."

The waitress snapped her gum. "Janice over there was a stylist before the dead started walking, if you're itching for a trim or scalp massage." She pointed at a woman with purple hair who was counting money on the countertop.

Shay touched her hair that was tied up in a messy bun. "New hair might be nice."

"I like your hair," Jed said.

"I look boring next to you." Shay ran a finger over his tattooed arm.

"No." Jed shook his head. "You're definitely not boring."

"Let's stay the night." Shay smiled wide. "We are almost to California. Just one last night with some normalcy."

Jed couldn't deny her, doubted he'd ever be able to. He wanted nothing more than a smile on her face. Shay had lost a lot these past few days. She'd fought for their lives and dragged Jed's lifeless body to safety. He'd give her the moon if he could. He looked down at his hands, tapped his fingertips together and sparks zipped between the pads.

"Maybe I could give you a haircut?" Jed suggested.

Shay laughed. "No thanks, cowboy. Leave that to the professionals."

When they finished eating, Shay went to speak to Janice about a haircut and Jed reserved the motel room. They met at the front door.

"Janice said she can do it now." Shay pulled the elastic holding her bun.

Jed leaned to the side and eyed the woman.

Shay smacked his arm. "Stop. Not everyone is a threat."

"Sure. Room twelve." Jed said with a dull tone and dangled the room key. "I'll go check out the room and meet you back here."

Shay kissed him on the cheek before turning around to follow Janice to the salon attached to the diner. It was a unique combination but Jed didn't dwell on it. Little towns like this typically had strip malls with random businesses. A diner and a salon didn't seem like such a bizarre combo after some things he'd seen on his travels. Tattoo shop and a comic shop. Massages and a dentist. It actually seemed a little normal here. Jed figured it was good for Shay to have a little normalcy.

Room twelve had two double beds and a tiny bathroom. Jed checked it over for markings. He searched for satchels of bones, piles of sand or salt, anything out of the ordinary. There was nothing. He breathed a sigh of relief, pulled a Sharpie out of his pocket, and drew a rune of protection into the top center of the doorframe.

He added a rune over each window and the bathroom door before heading back to the diner for more coffee and to wait for Shay.

He asked for the corner booth this time since the lunch rush was over.

The same waitress snapped her gum, nodded, and brought him to the table. Jed grabbed a newspaper off the newsstand as he passed.

"You still hungry?" She had a smile that led him to believe she'd give him more than food if he asked. It wasn't new. It also wasn't desired. His mother had used his face to get plenty of money and help them survive when he was a kid. He knew what his face could get him, besides killed.

"Just coffee," Jed said with an empty smile and a nod as

he opened the newspaper and began reading. He didn't want her to get any ideas that he might be interested. He wasn't.

The mug was chipped but the coffee fresh. Jed turned the pages of the newspaper, stopping when he saw an article about missing children. He continued reading.

"Sad story," the waitress tapped the paper as she refilled his mug. "That there is Jennifer Asheworth. Didn't live too far from here. Used to bring the kids in every Thursday for lunch."

"You knew them?" Jed asked.

"As much as a waitress can. Gave the kids free milk." She rested a hand on her hip and shook her head in despair. "Damn shame someone could kill a single mother like that and steal the kids. Especially in times like these."

Jed looked at the pictures in the paper. "They were kidnapped?"

"Some say poor Jennifer haunts these parts." The waitress popped a bubble. "You want some pie or something? All this coffee is going to give you the jitters."

The last bit was such a redirection of their conversation that Jed stared in disbelief for a moment before he said, "Sure."

"We got apple, pecan, or peach."

"Apple."

"Ice cream?"

"No thanks." Jed finished reading the article about the missing kids. He checked the date on the paper. It was a few weeks old. It did not surprise him it was old, news was scarce in all formats. Kinda hard to get the news out when everyone is too busy dying or defending themselves.

She brought him a slice of pie. It tasted sour. He slid the plate away and drank his coffee.

———

JED WAS ENGROSSED in the newspaper when Shay walked up to him. She stood at his elbow for a few seconds but all he did was hold out his coffee mug.

Shay took it out of his hand and set it aside. She ran her finger from his wrist up to the crook of his arm.

He was even more attractive like this; reading, drinking coffee, totally engrossed in something besides staying alive. So normal. Shay wondered if he'd ever really relaxed in his life.

When her fingertip made it to the sensitive skin of his inner elbow, Jed turned his head quickly and focused on her.

"Shay?" He was staring like he was seeing her for the first time.

"I might not have a blue aura like you, but now I have some blue. We match. A little." Shay touched her hair. Blowtorch blue was what Janice had called the color. "Do you like it?"

Jed scooted to the side and pulled her down next to him into the booth. "It suits you." He touched her hair. It was shorter than before, shoulder length but still manageable if she needed to put it up.

Shay smiled, warmth filling her center. She wasn't looking for acceptance. She'd change her hair if Jed liked it or not. But the way he was looking at her and the way his arm tightened around her back led her to believe she could dye her hair gray and he'd still be enamored with her.

"Hey, look at this." Jed directed her attention to the newspaper.

Shay read the article about Jennifer Asheworth and her kidnapped children.

"Is this the ghost woman?" Shay asked. "The lady in white?"

"Could be."

Suddenly, a yawn overtook Shay. She covered her mouth.

"You're tired." Jed motioned for her to get up. "Let's get some rest. Checkout is ten in the morning."

Jed was glad the diner and motel took money and hadn't switched to bartering. He didn't want to give up their supplies.

They stopped at the Jeep and got out their bags before heading to the room.

CHAPTER 4

Jennifer Asheworth was a single mother dealt a life of hard work and sacrifice, devoted to her children and the Roman Catholic Church. She'd survived most days on donations and the good will of others. She'd raised her children modestly and they found happiness in warm meals and clean beds. It was all Jennifer could have ever asked for; a simple life in the mountains.

She hadn't planned to navigate life alone. It was simply the cards she was dealt. She'd had love, but it had wilted and rotted like an over-watered rosebush. It was a hard pill to swallow, the day Dan had left her alone with the children. He'd left the state for opportunity and promised he'd send money. It never came. But, he'd given her the greatest gift, her children. Sarah and Jacob were enough for Jennifer and she poured her whole life into raising them. Many days were hard, but worthwhile.

When a handsome man started sitting near her in Sunday

church, she felt the way he gazed at her and smiled when she walked by. It had been so long since someone had paid attention to her. It had been years since Dan left. She didn't say no when the rugged man named Alastor asked her to dinner, and even invited her children. It was a whirlwind romance that ended in an unfortunate event near a valley stream.

That was the day Jennifer learned no woman was safe and her children even less so. Handsome men bring lies disguised as promised and unrequited danger.

Five men with red eyes came from the tree line. Fast. Dangerous. A dark energy seeped from them like nothing Jennifer had ever experienced.

"No!" Jennifer screamed as two of them grabbed hold of her little girl. Alastor gripped Jennifer and shook her, but a mother's strength is not to be reckoned with. She kicked Alastor in the crotch and ran for little Sarah, all the while screaming for Jacob to run away to safety.

There were too many of them. Sarah wasn't strong enough but she still fought, all the while wondering how her God could allow this to happen. Alastor grabbed Jennifer by the hair, kicked her feet out from under her, and held her under the cold water of the stream.

The last sound she heard were the screams of Sarah and Jacob as the men took them away.

Her soul never left the Earthen plane. She couldn't leave her children. She searched the forest, guided by their cries in the night. She followed the red-eyed men back to their camp and promised herself she'd destroy them, just as they'd destroyed her.

Jennifer tried to leave clues for the Sheriff. She followed the investigators assigned to her case and left bits of information. Nothing stuck. Everything was looked over and forgotten. Jennifer soon realized that nobody cared and justice would never be served. She'd spent plenty of time trying to be seen but no one saw her until that day Shay found her missing ring in the stream.

CHAPTER 5

Shay dreamed of Nero racing across the foothills of Montana, kicking up dirt as he ran faster and faster, blasting through wildflower clusters, petals flying everywhere. There were wild horses trailing him. Then there was snow. A whiteout. She couldn't see anything but snowflakes. She shivered and couldn't stop, it was so cold.

Shay woke up, the chill of the room seeping into her bones. She glanced at the other bed. Jed insisted on giving her space. If he were next to her, she wouldn't be cold right now. She thought of climbing into the other bed and snuggling up next to him. She wanted nothing more than to touch him. It was hard going throughout the day without touching him. She was drawn to him and Shay couldn't help but think there was more besides his good looks and height that drew her to him. He had a good heart. She knew that. Suddenly her mind was filled with thoughts of that night at the ranch when the Demons came and killed Momma, then when

Daddy turned and she jammed a knife into his skull. Shay felt the tears welling in her eyes and swallowed hard. She hadn't cried about losing her family since they left the ranch that day. Now that it had come to the forefront of her mind, she couldn't stop thinking about it. Grief swelled in her heart and she wiped at her eyes.

She glanced at Jed sleeping. She should go to him. But then, something white caught her eye. She saw movement near the door. Jed had used his marker to ward the room and lined the window and door with salt. Still, something glowed outside and illuminated around the doorframe.

Unable to sleep or ignore the light, Shay slid out of bed. Drawn by more than curiosity, she stepped into her boots, turned the lock on the motel room door, and went outside.

Shay shivered as the winter chill met her skin. Wishing she'd grabbed a jacket, she looked down and saw the ring she'd found by the water on her finger.

I don't remember putting that on, she thought. She'd tucked the ring into her pocket near the water. She never put it on her finger and she wasn't sure how it had gotten there now.

"Whatcha doing out here in the dark, little lady?" There was once voice, but five men.

Fuck, Shay thought to herself. Bad odds. She'd left her gun inside on the nightstand.

"Je–" before she could get out a scream, a hand clamped over her mouth. Shay struggled. She kicked and wriggled her body, trying to get loose, but the man holding her had an unnatural strength.

They carried Shay to a black van parked at the road. She kicked and bit and scratched but couldn't get free. Panic flooded her as her arms were jerked behind her back and tied with rough rope. It tore her skin. She struggled as hands forced her to the floor of the van. One boot stomped on the small of her back. A blindfold was stretched tight across her eyes. This wasn't good. Panic started filling her chest. It reminded her of all those times Clyburn trapped her in the root cellar or the barn or the garden shed. This was worse. Much worse.

The last thing she thought was she didn't want to die like this. She'd barely gotten to experience life outside of the ranch and Colstrip.

———

JED JERKED AWAKE. Something was wrong.

"Shay," he called. Her bed was empty, her boots gone from near the door. "No."

Jed ran out of the motel room, barefoot and shirtless. "Shay!" he shouted. There was nothing outside, just the chill of winter that had arrived, the small snowflakes that were falling from the sky, and an eerie silence. The clouds broke and moonlight illuminated the disturbed snow in the parking lot. Jed followed the footprints to the road. She'd struggled and fought. Of course she did. This was Shay, the toughest cowgirl he'd ever met. He knew she'd give hell to whoever took her.

Jed's fingers twitched and tapped and bent like a row of

pyramids. He whispered words that sounded like the darkest of promises. They sounded like *murder*. Slowly, an image appeared like a memory in the road. He saw a black van. The five men. And Shay, kicking one of them in the jaw.

That's my girl, Jed thought as he noticed there was something off about one man. He was tall, shadows danced along his face as though his skin was struggling to maintain its form. Jed saw the glint of sharp teeth, the flash of a red eye. Sickness tore at his gut. The van drove away.

There was a wavering figure against the snowscape across the road. It was the woman in white. She pointed down the road while staring at Jed. Jed nodded in understanding. Jennifer's ghost was going to help him.

Jed returned to the motel room to collect their belongings. He threw it all haphazardly in the back of the Jeep. He started the engine and took off, following the tire tracks in the snow until the snowfall became so heavy that the tracks disappeared.

Ahead, he saw the red glow of brake lights. He turned off the Jeep's headlights and trailed the van in darkness.

Chapter 6

They tied Shay up like a dog on a stake. There were three men testing the strength of the chain that was wrapped so tightly around her waist that it pinched her skin. She should have never left the motel room. She should have closed her eyes or crawled into bed with Jed and gone back to sleep. That would have been a much better scenario than the one she was in right now. Shay tried not to let her thoughts run off. Despair would get her nowhere. She needed a plan. She needed these men to know that she was a difficult prey, maybe even make them regret they'd stolen her in the night.

A man with an unkempt beard and Carhart coat walked toward her. Shay backed up, until the chain jerked taut. It was the ringleader. She could tell by the sound of his voice. She'd heard him giving orders in the van. There was something about him though, the way the hollows of his cheeks seemed to change in the light. It made her uneasy.

"Like what you see?" he asked with a leering smile.

"You're fucking disgusting," Shay spat at the bearded man.

"Just keeping humanity alive." He tossed a bottle of water within her reach. "Someone has to, why not us?"

Shay looked to her left and saw smaller tents that appeared empty. The leaves and snow weren't disrupted. A sickening feeling filled her gut when she noticed a child's shoe near the base of a tree.

Something terrible happened here. Something terrible would continue to happen here. She could feel it–an uneasiness in her gut, a vibe that was menacing encompassed the camp.

The bearded man walked away and helped the others by adding logs to a fire and setting a large pot to the heat. He gave more orders and the other men went off and did what he commanded.

At least they could boil water. Shay wondered if they'd feed her. She hadn't eaten since the grilled cheese at the diner the day before. It had been a full day without food. Shay shifted and sat cross-legged. She grabbed the bottle of water, twisted off the cap, and drank it. She was thirsty and her throat ached from shouting at the men. At least she got a good kick out and probably broke the guy's jaw. She watched them cook, then watched them eat from the open door of her tent. They didn't share.

Night came. Shay was freezing. She shuddered and pulled her arms into her thin shirt. The awful sleeping bag they'd given her smelled like someone else's sweat. Shay wasn't too proud. She knew the cold could kill her. She'd crawled into the sleeping bag and put it over her head. She hated she couldn't zip the tent fully closed because of the chain secured around her waist. These men were idiots. They didn't have the slightest idea how to survive out here. Her daddy, Nicholas, would roll over in his shallow grave if he saw this mess.

Shay's body ached from the fighting and the shivering. Rocks underneath the tent didn't help. She could smell the fire in the center of camp and gave up on the cold tent. She opened the zipper, dragged the sleeping bag outside, and got as close to the fire as her chain would allow.

There was one man keeping watch. His beard was red and eyes dark. A shotgun was propped against his knee.

Shay didn't think he deserved a conversation, so she focused on the burning coals and was thankful for the little bit of heat that made it to her. Curiosity won, though. She wanted to know what she was up against. Nicholas had always told her humanity would turn to shit pretty quickly, and it appeared to have done just that.

"You have children here," Shay said.

"Had." The man closest to her made a face like he couldn't care less. "We'll have more. They're worth a lot." He eyed her up and down. "Worth more than you."

"What do you do with them?" Shay sipped her water.

"Sell them. If they make it."

"If?"

"Keeping kids alive is harder than you think. Haven't found a woman to help us." The man watched her. "But now we have you."

Shay shuddered. These sick fucks. She knew she'd been lucky her whole life. She had parents who loved her and made sure she was safe. Shay's stomach turned. She'd seen newspapers and missing persons' reports her entire life. Too frequently children went missing. She couldn't help but wonder if this group of men with their peculiar leader had been doing this for a long time.

CHAPTER 7

Jed drove faster. Feeling the tires slipping on the snow coated road, he let his foot off the gas in hope to gain traction.

Not tonight, he told himself as he eased the Jeep away from the shoulder.

He could barely see the vehicle's taillights. The snow was coming down faster and the van was nothing more than a shadow, the taillights a pinprick of red. Jed accelerated down a stretch of road that was straight. His heart started beating harder, adrenaline was coursing through his body as he got closer. Then, suddenly, it was gone.

No, Jed thought to himself. He went faster; the wheels sliding, unable to grip asphalt through the layer of slick snow. A sign came into view. There was a turn. Jed let off the gas. The tire tracks from the van had taken a sharp left. Jed turned. He could feel the Jeep sliding. This wasn't good.

The Jeep skidded. Traction control kicked on and the

tires made a staccato motion trying to grip the road. It didn't work. The Jeep slid off the road, hit an embankment and rolled.

———

JED'S NECK and shoulders ached. His head felt full of fog. He blinked a few times, realizing he was hanging upside down by his seatbelt. Jed groaned, one arm searching for the buckle release. He hit it and braced for impact as he fell.

The windshield shattered. Cold air and snow blew into the Jeep. Jed was careful where he dragged his body, avoiding the glass shards. It was pitch black outside. He glanced at his watch. It was nearly four in the morning. He'd been out for at least two hours. Two hours was a long time for the van to get away. They could be in another state right now. Anger flooded Jed's body. He punched the passenger headrest. This is why he didn't involve anyone. They weren't safe. Next time, he'd tie her up. He bit his cheek imagining Shay tied to the bed with that blue hair spread over the pillow like a crown. Damn. No. No. Next time he'd ward the door so it wouldn't open without him.

Jed crawled to the back of the Jeep and dug through the supplies. He found some wipes in the bugout bag and used them to clean the blood off his face. Jed could feel tiny scrapes on his skin. He needed a moment to think, to plan.

Jed lay on his back, hands gripping his hair. He needed to find Shay but knew it would be pointless in this weather and cold. He could only hope whoever took her was keeping her warm. He would find them.

Jed thought of the woman in white. There weren't many who believed in magic and supernatural lore, at least nobody he came across. Except for the Crow family. Jed considered them. The grandmother seemed to be the most knowledgeable of the bunch. She'd said that she had her own magic. He recalled passing a sign for Hoopa territory. Maybe the Crow family had connections. Jed hadn't asked a soul for help since Declan died. He didn't like the feeling of depending on others. Actually, he hated the feeling.

Jed rolled his shoulders, relaxed his body, and prepared for the astral projection. He had to be careful, too much magic would bring attention. It would ignite his aura and while most humans couldn't see any difference in him, others would. Angels would see the blue from the sky and divebomb him. Demons would see the glow through the thinning veil and climb out of the ground after him. Jed's magic was a blessing and a curse, but also a necessity.

His fingers tapped in spell casting. He spoke words that sounded like an echo through time, like a whale song from under the deepest depths of the ocean. He closed his eyes, felt his body lighten, and when he opened them again he was standing in the backyard of the Crow residence.

Jed wasn't his whole form; he was something lighter, transparent. A ghost to the unknowing.

Grandmother Crow was rocking on the back porch. The squeaking of old wood paused. "What do you want, Allegewi?"

Jed paused for a moment noticing the blue light illuminating her. Jed had heard her saying some called her healing magic and now he wondered if she was just like him. A zapping noise brought realization it was just a blue-bug zapper light hanging from the porch railing.

"You can see me?" he asked.

"Of course."

"Can the others?"

"Possibly."

Grandmother Crow had the usual suspicious curiosity but she was unshaken at his appearance. "Why are you here?" She stood and moved closer, inspecting him. "You're not whole."

"I am elsewhere," Jed said. "I need help. Someone has kidnapped Shay."

Grandmother Crow wasn't one for words. Her expression was murderous. "How did that happen?"

Jed explained only what he knew. There was the ghost of Jennifer Asheworth haunting Shay and the van he was chasing.

"You should have left her with us. She'd be safer here," Grandmother Crow said.

"She wanted to come with me," Jed said. "Did you know her family is dead?"

"Yes." Grandmother Crow crossed her arms and shivered as she looked off into the distance. Her lips pressed into a thin line before she focused on him again and spoke. "There is something dark running through these parts and it's not the dead walking."

"There were Demons," Jed warned her. "I killed them."

"I sense there are more."

"There always are."

"As for the ghost. You must burn the bones or personal items and the haunting will stop. Release their souls."

"And the men who took Shay?"

"There must be a connection. That would be why she chose Shay."

"Why would she choose Shay? Why not me?"

Grandmother Crow smiled. "You'd not help a ghost. You'd blast a cannon of salt through its center and move on."

Jed knew she was right. He wouldn't have helped. He would have kept moving and minded his own business. "I need help finding them."

Grandmother Crow's gaze bore into Jed's soul. "You need little help, Allegewi. Unless it is protection from my son Hosa who still speaks of leaving home to hunt you down."

Jed made a face. "He's not the first."

"Go, Allegewi," Grandmother Crow waved. "The ghost will help you. Go back to your body," she waved, "before something dire happens to it."

Jed whispered a spell that returned him to his body. He inhaled a deep, strangled breath. His eyes focused. He was not alone.

Chapter 8

NERO RUBBED HIS FLANK AGAINST A TREE TRUNK. The scratch from the Crossroads Demon had become inflamed and wept black fluid. He rubbed the area around the scratch, draining the fluid before walking into the nearby lake to soak. The water was icy and felt good on the wound. Nero drank from the clear water. He'd crossed the veil again. The moon was less ochre here. On the other side of the veil, Nero noticed everything was darker. The shadows, the creatures, the dirt. He didn't think he'd like it there, but both realms were beginning to feel alike. Darkness was spilling over.

Shay was on this side. He could feel her. Their bond was stronger. That other thing was on this side of the veil too. Nero knew Clyburn had turned into something evil. He'd seen the man change, he'd seen Clyburn searching for Shay where they'd rested at the stream. Nero had watched Clyburn, then followed him.

A scream tore through the night. Nero's ears flicked upright. The voice was far away but he knew who it was. He felt it in his bones.

Shay.

Nero walked out of the lake and shook. He felt the pull through their bond. She was far away, further than he'd wanted.

Nero took off at a full gallop toward the scream. He ran through the night, past empty roads and frozen foothills. He leapt over downed trees and crashed cars blocking his path. The sun rose, the sun set. His hooves left imprints in the snow melt and mud. He didn't eat or drink; he ran as fast as he could.

Suddenly, their connection flickered. Nero slowed and stomped his hooves. Eyes wide, he took in his surroundings. There was a snarl nearby, the smell of a creature that used to be a man. Nero focused across the prairie.

Clyburn was there.

If the stallion knew anything, it was that Clyburn was still hunting Shay as well.

Darkness consumed Nero as a desire to protect Shay became overwhelming. Something like a roar rose out of Nero as he galloped toward Clyburn, ready to kill.

There was another scream in the distance.

Shay!

Clyburn turned and ran toward Shay's voice. The movement was eerie and rapid.

Nero followed.

CHAPTER 9

Jed's eyes finally opened and he took in a deep breath of cold air. There was something about his soul leaving his body that just felt wrong. The whole time, he had a feeling of detachment, emptiness, and an eagerness to return quickly. He'd only used the spell a handful of times but never to travel so far for so long. He didn't like it and desired to never do it again.

The sun was coming up. Jed was disappointed in himself that he'd taken so long to travel to Grandmother Crow. He stretched, cold and weary from draining his magic with the apparition spell. He was rusty with some of the magic that Declan had taught him.

Jed saw bone white feet and legs beyond the broken windshield. Jennifer's ghost was there. She was waiting patiently.

Grandmother Crow was right. He would have blasted

the ghost with salt and moved on. But now he needed Jennifer. He needed her to get Shay back.

Jed listened for any noise, rolled to the side, grabbed his bag, and crawled toward the broken windshield. He wanted to take a bugout bag but it would slow him down. Jed had his spell book and everything he needed in his leather bag. He'd lasted this long with minimal supplies.

The snow was past his ankles. Jed wasn't prepared for winter and hoped the snow would stop for the next few weeks. Dealing with the chill in the air of pending winter differed from dealing with full-blown winter. Jed dusted off his jeans and shirt.

"You know where she is?" Jed asked Jennifer.

She turned, her pale form blending with the snow. She pointed the way.

He shouldered his bag and headed down the road. Jed was tired from the spell he'd used to visit the Crow residence. He wished he had time to rest, but every moment Shay was in the kidnapper's hands was one moment closer to her death. A bitterness boiled in his stomach. He knew this would happen. He had to make Shay see she was better off without him.

CHAPTER 10

CLYBURN HAD ONLY STOPPED RUNNING ONCE TO fill his gut on a nest of squirrels. After, he followed the faint trail left by Shay. He'd run across mountains, foothills, and the western plains. Clyburn couldn't move as fast as the Jeep Jed and Shay were driving, but he could almost catch up each time they stopped. He came across Shay's strongest scent at a stream close to the road. Clyburn paced and inhaled deeply, doing his best to soak up every molecule of her scent that remained.

"Precious," Clyburn murmured to himself as he stood up straight, looking more man and less animal as he inspected the land around the stream, looking for clues. He wanted Shay, and he wanted the golden ring and bracelet. It all belonged to him. They could've dropped it. They wouldn't know how important it was to him. He turned over rocks and dug frantically at the pebbled stream, pausing when he found nothing. Clyburn scratched his head. Or maybe they knew, and that's why they took it. It wasn't here.

Sharp claws dug into the soil. Clyburn had the desire to draw an X and invite up some friends to help. He remembered what happened at the ranch and what the abomination half-breed did. Clyburn wanted to end Jed. Taking Shay would be enough revenge.

Moonlight illuminated the prairie. Clyburn saw a dark glimmer in the distance. Darkness. It moved. Clyburn dropped to the ground once again, looking like a beast on all fours. Something was following him. He sniffed the crisp breeze and recognized the animal.

CHAPTER 11

THE SLAP ACROSS SHAY'S CHEEK STUNG. SHE prodded the corner of her mouth with the tip of her tongue and tasted blood. Bastard.

Shay scrambled to her feet. She gripped the chain that hung from her waist and tested its weight. Her arms ached from fighting. Her body was cold and sore. She had too many bruises and scrapes to count. She'd gotten a few good hits in, but she was much smaller than the red bearded man. Brute was winning this fight, but Shay had one last trick up her sleeve.

He was close, shaking the sting out of his hand after hitting her. His back was to her ruined tent. The bastard had cut a hole in the side to surprise her. He wasn't expecting a fight, that's what she gave him. The scratch down the side of his face was bleeding. What Shay wouldn't do for her handgun or a heavy rope. Lord knows she'd rangled enough cows and horses. What was one stupid man to add to the mix? She was sure the cows and horses were smarter than Redbeard.

Shay swung the chain like a jump rope. Once, twice, three times before Redbeard noticed. Shay skipped to the side and swung, momentum looping the chain around his neck. Shay dropped to the ground and pulled tight. Redbeard fell, kicking at the frozen dirt and scratching at the chain around his neck.

"How do you like it, you fuck?" Shay spat out as she pulled the chain tighter. It jerked snugger around her waist as Redbeard struggled.

Redbeard yelled threats that were barely understandable as she crushed his windpipe. He rolled, twisting the chain and her arms. He grabbed her ankle and tugged, knocking her off balance. Shay rolled, her free ankle getting wrapped in the chain.

Redbeard still had a good grip on her other leg. His fingers were so tight she knew he'd leave bruises. Shay was cursing her shit luck as she rolled and scraped her tangled foot against Redbeard's knuckles.

The chain had loosened just enough for him to shout, "You bitch!"

That brought the cavalry. Suddenly, hands were on Shay, gripping her arms, throwing her back against the ground. A boot was at her neck, a large hand pulling her hair. The ringleader was wandering over, looking like he was annoyed.

Two men assisted Redbeard at getting untangled and to his feet. He rubbed his throat.

"What's going on here?" the ringleader asked.

Shay glared at Redbeard and struggled against the men holding her down. She was in a shit position on the ground like this and outnumbered. She was breathing heavy from the struggle and the boot on her throat.

The ringleader flicked his wrist and the men released her. "One girl did that to you?" he mocked Redbeard. "One little, pathetic girl. You're such a disappointment, Red. Get the fuck out of my face. All of you, move!"

Shay moved to her feet as the men left and scattered about the camp. Some went to the fire, others went to the cabins in the distance. Shay focused on the ripped tent. She'd prefer a cabin to sleeping on the cold ground. At least wooden walls would offer a little protection against these creeps.

"Sorry about that." The ringleader said as he inspected the ripped tent with the toe of his boot. "Wasn't supposed to happen."

Shay glared and tugged at the chain around her waist. She was calculating its length and judging if she could move fast enough to toss it around his neck. He wouldn't be too hard to strangle. The ringleader was a good bit taller than Redbeard, more muscular too. He'd probably put up a good fight. Shay didn't think too hard about it.

"Ah ah," the ringleader shook his finger at her. "Don't."

"Release me."

"Where would you go?" He walked closer. "It's dark. Cold. You're obviously frightened. If I released you into the night, who knows what could find you?" He flashed a smile and Shay was almost certain she saw sharp teeth. "A wolf, a bear maybe. Or something... darker."

Shay glared.

"I didn't properly introduce myself." He held out a hand. "Alastor."

"I'm not touching you." Shay seethed.

"That's your call." Alastor tucked his hands in his pockets, appearing nonchalant and unthreatening. Shay knew better. There was something not right about this man, from the shadows of his face to the sharp teeth she'd just seen. "I can help you with this transition."

"I'm not transitioning jack-shit."

Alastor chuckled. "You will." He took a deep breath and wandered the radius of where she'd been tied up. "If you want out of this set up, you'll transition. There's really no other option." He winked.

"To what?"

"One of us." Alastor said it so calmly, like Shay might know what the hell these men are.

"I refuse to kidnap children." Shay shook her head.

Alastor smiled. "You will help us. You have to."

"Nope."

Alastor moved quickly, just a few strides, and he was in Shay's space, his fingers gripping her chin and the chain near her hip. "I'd hate to see you turn into one of those walking corpses."

"I'm not afraid," Shay said, trying to move but she couldn't. Her body felt frozen in place. Fear prickled her spine and she couldn't look away from Alastor's black eyes.

"Your body tells me otherwise."

The chain snapped and fell away from Shay's hips. *Freedom*! Shay wanted to run but she couldn't. She felt frozen in place by some other force.

"Follow me," Alastor said as he released Shay's chin and began walking toward the cabin. "Since these men are so distracted by you, I'll have to keep you closer."

Shay followed him, against her will. Alastor walked her to the largest of the cabins and opened the door. Warmth greeted Shay. A roaring fire in a heating stove illuminated the corner of the cabin. There was furniture, a kitchenette, a separate bedroom, and a bathroom.

"Go," Alastor motioned to the fire as though it was the greatest gift ever given to her. "Get warm."

Shay moved past the man and dropped to her knees in front of the stove. She held her hands close to the heated glass. She didn't realize how cold she was after days of sleeping outside on the ground. Shay caught her reflection in the glass door of the stove. There was dirt on her face, her blue hair was disheveled, and leaves were tangled in the strands. She reached into her hair and began pulling out the leaves, crushing them in her free hand.

All she could think is she should have never left that motel room. Never. Tears stung her eyes. Shay hated the position she was in. Hated that it was her fault. There was something wrong with her to keep finding herself in these positions. She was stronger than this. Smarter, too. She wiped tears off her face and smeared the dirt and blood down her cheeks.

"Don't be upset," Alastor said. "It will get better." He crossed the room and motioned to the bathroom. "When you're warm take a shower. There's clean clothing and towels on the counter."

Shay pressed her lips together and swallowed against her sore throat. She wondered how many women they'd done this to. How many families they'd ruined. Shay had thought the walking dead were bad. This ugliness was worse, and to think they'd been around since before the dead started rising. Alastor certainly wasn't all human, but the other men were, and they were participating in this willingly.

She glanced at Alastor, noticed the light from the flames made his face look less angled and devious. Shay closed her eyes, squeezed her handful of leaves, and focused on the crunch of them against her palm. She needed a plan now that she was free of the chain. Her stomach grumbled. She hadn't eaten in days. It was a distraction. Shay needed to focus and plan.

"I'll make you something to eat," Alastor said from the kitchenette. It sounded so normal, so nice and non-threatening. He was playing a game. "I bet you're hungry."

Shay could play too. Maybe if she could gain his trust, she could get free. Shay stood and walked toward the bathroom. "Thank you," she said as she closed the door.

The bathroom was small but at least there were walls between her and Alastor and the other men. She started the shower and let the crushed leaves from her hand fall into the nearby trash basket. Shay reached for the doorhandle to lock it, only to find there was no lock. Her stomach churned. She didn't like that. Anyone could walk in if they wanted.

Shay toyed with the ring on her finger, took it off and set it on the bathroom countertop. There was something about that ring.

Shay turned on the shower and waited. She watched the door handle intently, waiting for it to turn. She waited five minutes. Pans clattered from the kitchen on the other side of the thin wall.

"There's only about ten minutes of hot water," Alastor shouted. "Soon it will be cold as a mountain stream."

There was nothing worse than a cold shower–besides the situation Shay was currently in. She undressed and got in the shower.

The water swirling around her feet was brown with dirt. Shay had never been so filthy, not even after a week of cattle driving. She was quick to wash and wrap herself in a towel.

Shay glanced at her reflection. There were bruises on her neck and arms from the manhandling. Scratches lined her face. She tilted her chin, remembering the deep cut across her forehead that Jed had healed. These shouldn't scar but they'd leave marks on her pale skin for a few weeks once they healed.

There was a set of sweats on the countertop. Cheap and nondescript. Shay dried off and got dressed. The sweats were oversized but she was clean and warm and thankful to be out of that filthy tent.

She took a deep, calming breath and opened the door. This was nothing more than a game, a game that could save or end her life. Shay reminded herself that she'd done it before that night she ran off and met Clyburn at the bar. She'd seduced him and it was easy. She told herself that she could do this.

CHAPTER 12

JED TRUDGED OVER CRUMBLING BLACKTOP AND thick mud from the snow melt. He watched the sky and the shadows of the forest, waiting for something to surprise him. Nothing other than squirrels and birds came. He was thankful for that. Jed tapped his fingers together in exercise. He didn't want his fingers to freeze up from the cold. He wanted his joints nimble and ready.

Jed's mind wandered the further he walked. He worried about Shay and what was happening to her. Thoughts of his fuck ups brought memories and soon Jed relived his time with Declan all those years ago...

Then

"Be gone with ya!" Declan shouted at the Demon.

The cloud roared and snapped, it undulated and twisted like a tornado. Thunderclap reverberated and drowned out Declan's voice.

Jed raised both hands and threw fire. "Run!" He shouted to Declan.

Declan rounded the dock and ran for the boat. "Hit the gas!"

Jed walked backward, but to get to the gas he'd have to stop throwing the fire. He shook his hands, dashed toward the gears, and accelerated. He ran back to the deck.

The boat was moving away from the dock, Declan was running full bore. Jed held out a hand and steadied himself.

Declan leapt, stopping midair as wicked jaws clamped down on his leg with a sickening crunch.

"No!" Jed screamed into the night.

Jed would never forget the look on Declan's face. The man smiled as his body hit the wooden dock. "I knew it would come one day." Declan's fingers tapped together and made a strange motion before the black cloud of teeth and talons consumed him.

Jed felt a bulge in his pocket as Declan vanished. He reached for it and pulled out Declan's spell book.

It filled Jed with anguish and hate as he strode to the engine room, pushed the boat into high gear and set toward Elk River, then the Atlantic.

There were plenty of places he could have stopped along his travels out of Chesapeake Bay. Little islands that only he could inhabit, plenty of rivers he could've followed until he found some small town to disappear in. He wanted to follow each idea that came to him. But, Jed remembered Declan had said, *"That's how I survived. They don't like the boats."* He took *a sip from the mug. "Or at least they didn't."*

Maybe taking to the water was Jed's best option at survival now? When the sun began to rise, Jed turned to see the smoke rising from Chesapeake City. He was sure most of the town had burned during the night. The Demon cloud probably tore it apart and ate its fill. He instantly wished to go back in time to the safety of Peabody Library. They should've stayed after its closing but Declan didn't want to break any rules or get caught.

Jed steered the boat around an oncoming fishing boat that was headed north. He waved to the crew and faked a smile as the fishermen onboard pointed to the dark smoke in the distance.

Jed couldn't look again, he could only focus on the sunrise and the open mouth of the Bay ahead of him. He'd coast out into the Atlantic and get lost amongst the waves and clouds. He could fish, he could find water, he needed nothing else.

It turns out, living on the ocean was incredibly lonely but Jed soon realized he didn't put others in harm's way. Demons didn't crawl out of the ocean to hunt him. Angels didn't drop out of the clouds onto the boat deck trying to send his tortured soul to the Astral plane. No, living on the sea was safe and it gave him time to practice the runes and the spells in the book Declan had sent him. Jed became quite good at it, practicing day after day, memorizing everything Declan had written down.

But, as life would have it, soon it became harder to open his eyes in the morning, fishing for breakfast and dinner became an unbearable chore, setting up the water containment during rain became an insufferable task–even as Jed's throat burned with thirst. When water rolled over the hull and the motion of the boat threw him from his bed, Jed simply rolled onto the floor and let the ocean that had invaded his boat cover him. He had been on the run for so long, that simply not running was too easy. There was no effort in it. This became a problem on its own. For darkness has a quicksand-like pull. It's slow, enveloping; the comfort of a firm embrace, the warmth of a mother's bosom pressed against her child's cheek. Jed had spent so long running from the darkness that surrounded him that he never took the time to explore it. Maybe the darkness was all that he needed, all that he desired, all that he wanted. Maybe the Demons and Angels were right to hunt and try to kill him. Water sloshed against his cheeks, and Jed tapped his fingertips against the book in his front pocket. It couldn't go with him. But, he'd spent so much time at sea it didn't matter anymore. There was nothing left for him in this life. Survival wasn't worth all that he'd thought. It had been years of only him and the salty air. He wasn't sure it was worth it any longer.

Jed closed his eyes as the water splashed over his eyes. He could see Declan again, he could see Eileen, he could see his mother. It was easy, simple, no effort. All Jed had to do was *let go*.

He felt himself slipping. Slipping and drifting and rocking into an abyss he'd never experienced before. It felt so… calming.

The water turned to ice. Jed sucked in a breath and sat up. The thin layer of ice crackled and broke, falling away from his body. He wasn't alone.

"Jedediah James Porter," a familiar voice whispered. "I never thought I'd see the day you gave up on life."

Jed focused on the corner of the room and saw the wavering spirit of his mother, Clara. Water sloshed over his knees as he rubbed his eyes.

"Have you not seen a spirit in all of these years?" Clara smiled as she moved closer to him, her dress disappearing under the water. "You saw them frequently as a child."

"I did?" he asked. He never remembered.

His mother nodded. "Most are harmless. I told you that once. Do you remember?"

"I don't."

"Son?" Clara's face was flexed in concern. "What exactly are you doing here?"

"I was sleeping." Jed cleared his throat.

"Sleeping under water?" She motioned to the open door. "In the middle of the ocean. Alone."

"It was peaceful."

"So is a summer breeze." She crouched, eye to eye with him. "I spent my life keeping you alive. Teaching you how to live. This is not living and you are far too young for death. I did not die for you to end up like this."

Jed's eyes burned. He was too dehydrated for tears. Salt crusted his face and hair. His clothing was frayed too thin.

Clara reached out a hand. "You must live. Even though you've lost."

He could feel her cold skin as she touched him. She had been warm when he was a child. Warm and soft. This feeling was too different.

"I may have died but I haven't been gone." Clara moved again. "I've been watching you when I can."

Jed blinked. He wasn't sure if he could believe his eyes or his mind. Plenty of illusions presented themselves on the ocean. Land, birds, fish. "You were young when you died," Jed said.

"I had lived. I had duty." Clara settled her hand on the helm. "You need to go back to the land. It's not right to be floating out here in the nothingness alone." Clara turned the boat.

"There's no gas." Jed ran a hand through disheveled hair and salt fell down his face as it came loose from the strands. "I burned through the last of it months ago." Jed stood and small chunks of ice fell off his body, melting in the water at his feet. "The sails."

Jed went to work setting the sails to catch the wind and bring him back to the mainland. His muscles ached, throat burned, and he was hungry but somehow he found the energy for the task.

Clara watched from the helm room.

After he set the sails, Jed went to work the manual bilge pump and get the water off the boat. He should have pumped the water off sooner. Now it had soaked in. He doubted he'd made it to the mainland before warping and mold destroyed the boat.

"You can fix it," Clara said, interrupting Jed's thoughts. She wiggled her fingers.

Jed looked down at his hands, calloused and rough. It had been a long time since he practiced magic. Somehow, survival had become more important. Jed searched his memories for the last time he'd tried a spell or felt the heat in his fingers as energy arced, eager to force change at his will.

"I'm not sure I can remember," Jed said.

"It's in your bones, son. You had it as a child before you ever knew a spell or the word magic. You've always had the *luck*."

It was true. He had the memories of opening locks and turning over engines and asking for coins in his cup. It always came and helped them survive life on the run together. But his luck had run out that night on the train when Clara sacrificed herself to a Demon and died. His luck ran out when that monster had tracked Jed's scent to Eileen's apartment and tore her apart. His luck ran out when the cloud Demon took Declan.

"If I go back to the mainland, I'll die," Jed said. "There's nothing for me there."

"You are many things, but a teller of the future you are not." Clara smiled. "There is plenty for you. Life, friendship, love." Her eyes twinkled with excitement. "You're so close, son." Clara's fingers drifted over the runes etched into the doorway and the helm. "Did you ever think that maybe you were meant to save someone?"

"Everyone has died."

"Not everyone, son. You haven't lived long enough to find out." She turned and focused on the sail as the wind blew. The boat picked up speed.

"Did you do that?" Jed asked.

"Never," Clara said. "As luck has it, you needed wind in your sail and someone gave it to you."

"Who?"

Clara shrugged.

"Who, mother?"

"If I knew who I could tell you, but I can only see so much from the Astral plane."

"You're not in Heaven?" Jed asked.

"Heaven is for some, just not me." Clara motioned to the ocean behind them. "You've read enough to know something isn't quite right with the record keeping."

Jed nodded. "There is no Heaven?"

"There's a Heaven, but a certain Archangel won't let me in." Clara smiled gently. "It's okay though. It means I can keep an eye on you. I have autonomy in the Astral."

"My father." Jed took a step closer. "Which one is he?"

Clara pressed her lips together.

"I deserve to know who sends the Angels down to try

and kill me. I deserve to know the one who hunts me from the heavens. Which one is my father?"

"If I say his name, I must go." She took in a breath she didn't need. "I'm not ready to go back yet. I want more time with you."

"You'll tell me before?" Jed asked.

Clara blinked and focused on the lapping ocean.

CHAPTER 13

ALASTOR WASN'T MUCH OF A COOK, IT APPEARED. But he'd managed pasta with jarred sauce. Shay didn't complain that the tomatoes weren't homegrown like the sauce Mamma had made on the ranch. She realized she'd never have sauce like that again. It hurt her heart; every realization that life would never be the same, that she would always miss two people in her life. Three if she counted Nero.

"Are you going to eat?" Shay asked Alastor as he crossed the room.

"Nope. Got things to do." He shrugged on a jacket and reached for the door. "Keep the fire going. You can have the bed." He opened the door and the chill of the night air blew in. He glanced at her before leaving. "Don't try to run," he said, voice deep and gravelly. "I'll find you."

Shay swallowed hard as he closed the door. No way in hell would she be sleeping in his bed. She was glad to be off the frozen ground but not that glad.

Shay stirred the pasta and sauce, wary that it probably wasn't just an innocent meal. There could be poison or drugs mixed in. She wanted to devour the entire bowl and was so hungry she could probably eat an entire box of pasta. Shay had to keep it together. She couldn't be getting drugged–then she'd never make it out of here.

Shay pushed her chair back and searched the kitchen. There wasn't much there; a few pots and pans, some plates, bowls, and silverware. Everything was boxed or canned or jarred from the grocery store. Shay wasn't surprised. Out here in the mountains she was sure everything was scarce. She searched every cabinet, even under the sink. She didn't find any chemicals or poisons. Something didn't sit right with her. Shay rubbed her sore face as she glanced out the window. It was snowing again. She'd left her boots near the bathroom door and now had an urge to put them on and run for the hills. But, she remembered Alastor's promise. She was sure he'd find her. She needed a different plan.

Shay drank water from the tap and found a box of crackers in the back of the cabinet. She imagined the dry, salted crackers tasted like warm pasta. When she was done, she put on her boots and walked to the front door. She turned the handle and felt the icy wind seep in.

The fire where the men sat was a few hundred yards away; close enough to smell the creosote, far enough that she couldn't tell if it was Redbeard sitting by it. She could only see the large man's body turn to watch her, then the red glow in his eyes.

What the heck, Shay thought to herself as she slammed the door closed.

Shay rubbed her eyes and tried to make a connection between everything she'd seen. There was evil here, she could feel it. She thought about the red eyes of some men and the shifting shadows of Alastor's face. Shay would have thought she was crazy a year ago, but now she knew better. She'd seen things that made little sense. But now she knew. These weren't real men. They were Demons.

Shay scrambled, searching the drawers for a marker or something to write with. She finally gave up and took a knife off the counter. Shay went back to the door and began carving. Jed hadn't given her any lessons in the runes or what they meant. She'd only watched him make the shapes over every doorway. Shay tried her best to remember every angle and curve. She took a chair from the table where her bowl of food cooled, uneaten, and used the chair to reach and mark the top of the doorframe. She wasn't sure she could outrun these men, especially not knowing where she was.

When she was done, her arm ached from carving with the paring knife. Shay tried not to be too hard on herself, but the runes looked like shit. She doubted they'd do much. She went to put the knife away, stopped midway, and hid it in her boot.

Shay sat in front of the fire and waited. She watched the orange and blue flames. She had an urge to run, to plan, to do *something*. But she was frozen in indecision.

Shay picked at her nail. Daddy would be so disappointed.

CHAPTER 14

____

THEN

JED MADE IT TO THE MAINLAND. THE STOLEN BOAT was unrecognizable by anyone in port, the paint sanded off by the salty air from years at sea.

"You made it," Clara smiled. "I knew you would." Her image had become more and more transparent. She was nearly invisible now.

"You feelin' all right, buddy?" a man asked from the docks.

Jed stared. He couldn't find the words to say. It had been so long since he had to hold a conversation with another living person.

The man held out a hand. "Throw me your rope. Are you alone?"

Another man was there. "He looks to be in shock."

"He looks sick," the first man said.

"Goodbye, son," Clara's voice was an echo.

"Wait," Jed's heart was beating fast. He needed to know. "Who was he?"

"Michael." Clara was gone.

Jed fainted.

Thankfully, the men at the port didn't call the law, instead they took Jed to a tiny, rural hospital that didn't ask many questions.

"You're drier that the Sahara," an old nurse slapped his arm, searching for a vein to poke. Salt crusted off his arm when she rubbed it with an alcohol swab. "How long were you lost at sea?"

Jed blinked, unsure of what to say. He was sure she wouldn't believe him. Five years, two years, ten years, twenty, he wasn't sure. He'd stopped counting. In the time that he was gone, things had changed in America. Cars honked in the streets, computers filled the nurses' station. It seemed technology had blossomed while he was gone. There were no horses, no dirt-packed roads, no long skirts or bowler hats.

"Forgot your words, honey?" the nurse poked his arm. Jed felt the sharp needle pierce his skin. "Jeeze, I expected dust to flow back." The nurse leaned closer to his arm. "Your blood is thick as sludge." She connected a tube to his arm. "We'll get you hydrated and get you out of here." The nurse stood and pressed buttons on an IV pump. "Want a turkey sandwich?"

Jed nodded.

He drank seven ginger-ales, ate four sandwiches, and the nurse pumped four liters of fluid into his vein.

Afterwards, he felt better but still sad. Still lonely. Still worried about causing the death of others.

The curtain moved and his nurse popped in to ask, "Hey, hon, a lady from registration is here to get your insurance information. Did you bring that with you?"

"I don't have insurance," Jed said, his voice sounding unfamiliar.

"I thought so." She stepped into the room and closed the curtain. "I brought you some clean clothes since yours are nearly see-through. This lady from registration," the nurse seemed concerned, "she can help you with other things, connect you to social services and help you get food and living arrangements."

"I don't need help," Jed said as he accepted the clothes.

"Didn't think so." She paused at footsteps outside the curtain. "Let's get you to the shower. I'll have her come back later."

Jed was grateful for the hospital shower and soap. The nurse had given him a razor but his beard was too thick. He could use a pair of scissors. He did his best getting cleaned up and left the bathroom feeling refreshed and ready to resume the challenge of life.

"Well you clean up nice, honey." The nurse smiled widely and looked him up and down. "Very nice. Do you have someone coming to pick you up?"

"No." He watched her, fascinated with the way she looked at him and licked her lips.

It had been a long time since a woman devoured him with her eyes. Previously, he would have shied from it. Today he reveled in it. The attention was giving him energy and hope. It made him feel alive again. He smiled back at the nurse as he tucked the spell book into the pocket of his new pants. He didn't need magic to charm. That had always come naturally to him.

"I feel a lot better, thank you," Jed said.

Dinner turned into a new pair of boots and a haircut and shave at the local barbershop. By the time Jed was done using up his luck, he felt filthier than the moment he arrived back on the mainland. He didn't like using people this way.

Still, he needed time to prepare and plan and the kind-hearted nurse offered her spare bedroom after she'd taken him to dinner. Jed agreed and paid off his debt in other ways before leaving on his own. He fixed a few broken cabinet doors, changed lightbulbs, hammered nails into the stairs until they stopped squeaking. When she took him to bed, he didn't say no. Payment with his body was easy and a simple tax, it was the least he could do for her compassion.

After all that; the battle, the ocean, his mother, he had a purpose now. He wasn't sure when he'd find the one he needed to save but at least he knew his time would come. And he knew which Archangel he'd kill. Michael.

———

Now

The winter wind was icy, and Jed was glad that no snow came with it. He'd been walking for days, searching for Shay.

Jennifer's ghost had been pointing him in certain directions but he was wondering if she didn't know where the van had taken Shay. He'd walked so far into the forest that he hadn't seen a road in a long time. Jed thought to use a spell to help him, but he'd used so much magic visiting Grandmother Crow that he was depleted.

A stick broke. Jed turned his head and saw the familiar ninety-degree bend of a tree branch. His gut sank. He was on reservation land. More sticks broke. Jed held up his hands.

"You got me, although it was an accident." He heard a voice, sensed movement. "I'll just go back."

A man with pitch-black hair stepped out into the open. "No, Allegewi, you will not go back." It was Jacy.

"Wonderful." Jed sighed and wondered for a moment if he should just embrace death when Hosa made himself known.

"When I went to your mother for help, I wasn't requesting help in killing myself." Jed made a face.

Hosa scraped a finger across his neck in silent threat.

"We didn't come for you," Jacy said. "We came to help locate Shay."

"Good." Jed adjusted his pack. "I haven't been able to find where they took her."

"You can't track," Hosa sneered. "Worthless creature."

"Not on my skills list," Jed said.

Jacy was already kneeling and inspecting clusters of leaves and low branches. "That way." He pointed.

"It's just the two of you?" Jed asked.

"There's more, close to here." Jacy said. "If we need them."

"Perfect," Jed whispered to himself.

"This way," Jacy motioned and began walking silently through the forest.

Jed felt like a bull in an antique shop. He made so much noise compared to the other two men. He was tired and didn't want to draw on his magic to conceal himself like he'd usually do when danger was near.

"Mother said you'd been following a ghost," Jacy said.

"She told me to," Jed said.

A shadow blocked the dappled light from the tree canopy. Jacy held up his hand and hushed the others.

Jed recognized the feeling instantly. Something had broken through onto the Earthen plane. Something had fallen or flown in to hunt him.

"It's an Angel," Jed warned, taking a knife out of his belt and stretching his fingers.

"I told you he'd bring more. He'd bring war to us," Hosa seethed.

"It's not my friend." Anger was coming off Jed in waves. "It's here to kill me."

For the first time since he'd met Hosa, the man was speechless. He didn't spit hateful words about Jed being an Allegewi and the war he'd bring upon them.

"The war has always been against me," Jed said. "I'm going to use magic to hide us." Jed tapped his fingers and uttered words that sounded like crackling ice. He turned invisible. Jacy and Hosa soon followed.

The Angel dropped from the sky. Like chiseled marble, the man landed on a bent knee and steadied himself. The ground shook with his landing.

Jed stood still near a thick redwood. He'd seen Jacy and Hosa ready themselves on the other side of the Angel.

"I know you're here," the Angel said. "I saw the blue light. You were glowing like a torch." The Angel turned, crushing frozen leaves under his feet. "You should really put a damper on that."

The Angel was looking in Jed's direction. He had a blade ready in his hand. He walked closer to where Jed was hiding, his eyes searching. There was movement behind the Angel.

Jacy and Hosa were moving. Jed figured they were probably leaving him to deal with the Angel himself.

The Angel spun and started marching toward the movement.

"Leave them," Jed said as he ran behind another tree, trying to distract the Angel.

The Angel turned again. He scanned the trees, looking for where Jed's voice came from.

Jed crouched and grabbed a fallen pinecone. He tossed it, then sprinted away. His magic was weakening. He knew he was flickering, and his invisibility spell was running out. He focused all the energy on hiding Jacy and Hosa and showed himself.

"There you are." The Angel ran full-bore at Jed, blade drawn and ready to chop.

Jed braced himself, pulling the heavily runed knife from his cargo pocket.

Jed held his own in battle, chanting spells, and jabbing with his knife when opportunity arose. The two men watched, unbelieving.

In the heart of the wintry forest, the air crackled with anticipation as Jed faced off against the Angel. His wings shimmered like freshly fallen snow in the dim light filtering through the frost-laden trees.

Jed stood, waiting, his eyes ablaze with arcane power. Snowflakes began swirling around him as his incantations filled the frigid air. He summoned tendrils of mystical energy, weaving them into a shimmering barrier that encircled him protectively.

The Angel radiated an ethereal glow and hovered gracefully above the frozen ground. His eyes were pools of narrowed determination as his blade glowed with pure light, its edges gleaming with divine energy.

With the flick of his wrist, Jed unleashed a barrage of arcane bolts, streaking through the air toward the Angel. He deftly dodged, weaving between the trees with effortless grace, his wings leaving trails of glistening frost in his wake.

Undeterred, Jed tapped into the elements, commanding the very essence of the winter surrounding them. Using all of his power, he had to reveal Hosa and Jacy. Icy winds howled as he conjured shards of ice, sending them hurtling toward the Angel.

The Angel's movements looked like a dance, a symphony of grace and purpose. With a swift flourish, he swung his radiant blade, dispersing the oncoming ice shards with a shower of crystalline sparks.

The forest seemed to hold its breath; not a creature moved or made sound, not a leaf fell. There was silence as the battle raged on.

Jed and the Angel's powers intertwined and clashed. It was a spectacle of light and energy. Jed's incantations grew louder, his gestures and fingers tapping more fervently, channeling energies beyond mortal comprehension. Energy he hadn't called upon in many years.

The Angel remained steadfast, swooping down with a divine power none had ever seen. Before Jed could finish with his spell, the Angel grabbed Jed, intending on taking him to the air. Jed would be useless in the sky. He'd been there before. Gravity was a force he couldn't control.

He worked his spell louder, faster. He clawed and pushed at the Angel's hands then dropped to the ground, kicked out a leg, and kicked the Angel off his feet.

Suddenly, Hosa was there with a hunting knife, Jacy as well. Jacy jabbed a knife into the Angel's shoulder as Hosa began chopping at the Angel's wings, his face twisted in a rage like never before.

Jed moved to his feet. He searched the fallen leaves for his knife that he'd dropped.

The Angel fought and yelled. Jed's spell was working at keeping the creature grounded. He whispered words that sounded like liquid metal flowing. Roots came out of the ground and held the Angel in place.

The Angel roared as Hosa removed a wing.

"You aren't supposed to be displaying those on the Earthen plane," Jed said as he moved to stand over the Angel.

"I'll display whatever I want as I kill you." The Angel was full of vitriol.

Jed palmed his knife before slamming it into the Angel's heart.

Bright celestial light illuminated the Angel's body as it died.

Jed shielded his eyes.

Hosa stood, the severed wing weighing down his hand.

Jacy cleaned his hunting knife on the Angel's clothing. "You been running from monsters like this?"

"Since the day I was born," Jed said. "Some get a little too close for comfort." Jed shivered as adrenaline coursed through his body.

Hosa was listening intently.

The Angel's body turned to ash, including the severed wing in Hosa's hand. "Allegewi," Hosa looked up, dismayed, "I was wrong."

Jed said nothing. He didn't need the apology, he only needed to know if Hosa would stop threatening to kill him.

"You know, Allegewi, the old stories of our people always said that the half-bred Angels were the demons. But now I am wondering if it was the Angels all along." Hosa held his open palm up and ash blew away in the icy wind.

A woman's scream rang out. The three men turned in the direction where it was coming from.

"Shay!" Jed started running.

CHAPTER 15

"This way," Jacy motioned for the others to follow as he veered around a thick cluster of trees and shrubbery.

The forest was dark, as daylight turned to night. Jed could see the light of a fire in the distance.

Hosa slowed and pointed to a trail marker. "We're off reservation land." He looked nervous.

"We get Shay out of there," Jacy said. "We owe it to Nicholas. We owe it to Shay."

They slowed and watched as they took Shay to a cabin. She was filthy, and Jed's body filled with rage when he saw the silhouette of tents in the distance.

"Calm yourself, Allegewi," Jacy warned. "Save that energy for the battle to come. We'll get her out of there."

Jed knew Jacy was right. He took a few deep breaths and closed his eyes, centered himself, and calmed. "How do you want to do this?" Jed asked.

Before them, a large fire roared in the center of the camp, casting dancing shadows that licked at the edges of the frozen trees. They waited patiently.

A man left the cabin where Shay was being held. Jed's heart pounded, the urgent need to rescue her echoing in the silence.

"We could just get her out through that window," Jacy said as he pointed. "Avoid those men."

"If they're men," Jed said. He'd learned to question everything and there was something about the glimmer in their eyes that told him those weren't true men.

Near the cabin, a silvery silhouette wavered. Jennifer was back.

"The ghost," Hosa warned.

"She's helping me." Jed repositioned himself, ready to move.

"Wait." Jacy grabbed Jed's arm. "Don't go running in there. That ghost only guided you in circles back there."

"How do you know?" Jed asked.

"We watched." Jacy made a face. "It needs to be sent away."

There was movement again. The door to the cabin opened. Shay was there, clean and dressed in fresh clothes. Whatever she saw made her quickly close the door.

"Create a diversion." Hosa pointed to the far end of the camp. "Get them away from the cabin, then run in and get her out."

"They'll follow," Jacy warned. He turned to Jed. "Have enough juice left in you for this?"

Jed was fatigued, but adrenaline kept him moving. He'd drain every molecule of magic out of his body if it meant getting Shay to safety. "I'm good," Jed replied.

With the twisting and tapping of his fingers, Jed summoned the bitter wind to howl through the trees, creating a cacophony that echoed through the camp. It sounded like hounds or a bear or some other dangerous creature. The Demons moved from where they rested, one by one, the noise drawing their attention away from the fire and the cabin.

Jed nodded to Jacy. "You go get her. I'll keep this up."

Jacy moved like a panther in the night, headed toward the cabin.

"This noise will bring the dead," Hosa warned.

Jed glanced to Hosa, wary. "There's a large horde of them close to here. Maybe twenty miles south, moving like a gathering storm and headed for this area."

Hosa's face turned grim. "Let's get this over with."

"Call the others," Jed warned.

"Not yet." Hosa shook his head. "We wait until the last moment."

Jed maneuvered around the trees, focusing his magic, drawing more men from their tents and cabins.

Jacy was crouched behind the cabin. He tried the window, but all the men realized now that Jacy was next to it. The window was far too small for anyone to escape through. Jacy moved to the corner of the cabin, watching for an opportunity to make it to the front door.

Jennifer's ghost was lingering, drawing attention from a large man near the fire.

"That ghost is going to give us away," Hosa warned.

"There's salt in my bag," Jed said, magic crackling in the frosty air as he unleashed bolts of icy energy, momentarily freezing a man who had appeared behind Jacy.

Hosa was digging in the bag until he finally pulled out a sealed bag of salt. "You carry this around for making soup?"

Jed smirked. "Take a handful and go throw it at the ghost."

Hosa ran across the camp and threw the salt like a pitcher in a baseball game. Jennifer's ghost disappeared, but the action caught the attention of someone else. Someone bigger and darker than anyone in the camp.

Jed took note. The man was a giant, the same one he'd seen take Shay to the cabin. But now he saw the man for what he really was. Shadows danced across his face, danced across his body as he transformed. His eyes glowed red. That was a pure-blooded Demon. Jed rethought their entire plan. This wasn't good. The other men were lesser Demons or possessed or a little bit of both, but this guy was massive. He pointed at Jed. A threat, a game plan. Jed instantly thought he'd rather take Hosa's murderous gaze any day over this guy's glare.

Jacy ran up to the cabin door and shoved it open. He ran inside.

Hosa was suddenly fighting with the man Jed had frozen.

The Demon took note before running toward the cabin door.

Jed's distraction at the far end of the camp wavered as he focused on the cabin. He ran out from under the cover of the trees.

The Demon threw open the cabin door but halted. He took a step to walk into the cabin but a force prevented him from going inside.

Pride flourished in Jed's chest. Shay must've learned some runes. She must've done something in there.

Jed cast a spell of protection on the cabin.

The giant Demon sensed the power then turned and smiled at Jed.

Jed paused.

The Demon raised his arm and pointed. Near the fire, the ground opened up. Dirt fell away and hands reached up. Bodies crawled out.

"Oh, shit," Jed said to himself as he watched a handful of lesser Demons crawl out of the ground. At least these were smaller, the size of cats and dogs. Fighting them would be like crushing ants. But they would keep coming in over-whelming numbers. The giant had to go down.

Jed reached for his belt, removing two knives and grip-ping one in each hand.

Chapter 16

In the shroud of darkness, where the night held its breath and the stars were veiled, Jed stood facing the towering Demon. A colossus of malevolence, its form cloaked in shadows and eyes aflame with infernal fury.

"You don't belong here, half-breed," the Demon said.

"I could say the same about you." Jed gripped his knives, looking for a soft spot. "What's your name?" he tried distraction.

"Your little human woman will be screaming Alastor later." The Demon smiled, revealing sharp teeth.

Jed stood resolute, his silhouette outlined by a faint aura of crackling blue energy. His eyes glowed with an otherworldly light. The magic that pulsed in him grew with his anger. Grew with his pain as memories of everyone he loved dying by the hand of Angel or Demon pulsed into his mind.

Alastor bellowed a guttural challenge that reverberated through the bleak landscape. He appeared to grow. His immense form loomed over Jed, casting a chill that seeped into the very fabric of the night.

With the flick of his fingers, Jed summoned arcane sigils that danced round him like ethereal flames, forming a protective barrier against Alastor's encroaching malevolence. The air crackled with anticipation, the tension thick enough to slice through the darkness.

Alastor lunged forward, his hands turned to claws, and swiped through the air, aiming at Jed. With a swift sidestep, Jed narrowly skirting the attack, his movements were guided by a grace born of a lifetime evading creatures like the one that stood before him.

Jed released a torrent of mystical energy, hurling bolts of crackling power at the Demon.

Alastor lunged forward, raw power and primal rage clear. A massive claw struck Jed in the side, sending him flying across the camp. Dirt and debris tore up Jed's back as he slid.

"We are outnumbered," Hosa warned from where Jed had landed.

"Get in the cabin," Jed said. "It's safe."

Hosa ran, leaving Jed to face the Demons alone.

Jed uttered words that sounded like crashing waves. He wove intricate patterns in the air with practiced precision, spells he hadn't used since that time he spent in the ocean with no one to harm but himself. Arcane tendrils erupted from the ground, the dark tendrils wrapped around Alastor and squeezed.

Alastor roared, his claws scratching at the shadowed tendrils. Jed moved to his feet, his back aching. Blood trickled down his spine. Pain brought power. In a crescendo of unfathomable brilliance, Jed unleashed a surge of blinding light. The light engulfed Alastor, searing through his ethereal form with a cleansing fervor.

With a deafening roar that echoed through the night, the Demon dissipated, his form unraveling into fading wisps of darkness that dispersed into the ether.

Jed stood, panting, his fingertips zapping with blue energy, his form bathed in the fading glow of blue light.

The battle wasn't over. Jed had defeated Alastor, but there were more men, possibly possessed, and the lesser Demons crawling out of the hole in the ground. He took in his surroundings. The cabin pulsed with a protection spell, but that didn't stop the lesser Demons from running toward it like ants to sugar. They swarmed, defying the gravity of the Earthen plane, crawling up the walls and across the roof, searching for a way inside.

CHAPTER 17

ELSU AND IYE WAITED ON SACRED RESERVATION land where it was safe. They watched for the signal from Hosa or Jacy, knowing that it might never come. This was a simple rescue mission, one the Grandmother Crow didn't want to send all four of her sons on. But the men knew there was strength in numbers, and the Allegewi would bring about things they'd never seen before. All of them had seen the disaster at the Dunn ranch. From the dark blood to the burning bodies to the strange markings on the thresholds of the doors and windows. The Allegewi was trouble.

A scrambling and scratching sound echoed in the night. Both men focused on the direction of the sound. The shadowed figure of a four-legged creature crouched and running, joints angled strangely, ran across the nearby prairie.

The sliver of moonlight revealed another figure; the inky shine of a black horse chasing the creature.

It was like nothing they'd ever seen before.

"I don't have a good feeling about this," Elsu said. "That horse..."

"Looks like Shay's horse." Iye was squinting and pointed. "What's that other creature?"

"Looks like a man."

The moon came loose of the clouds and the creature ran across an open field.

"That's a man. Or it was once a man," Iye said.

"That's Clyburn." Elsu said. He looked at his brother with determination. "We go now."

Without words, the men knew something dire was coming. They'd heard the woman screaming and soon they'd hear the roaring of a Demon taking its last breath on the Earthen plane.

Iye and Elsu got on their horses and galloped after the dark duo. Everyone headed toward the scream that had invigorated the night.

Chapter 18

"Hosa!" Shay said as the door to the cabin burst open.

Hosa slammed the door closed and leaned his back against it as though something might try to blast through at any moment. He was out of breath and gore stained his arms.

"The Allegewi said this is the only safe place," Hosa surveyed the cabin, his eyes stopping at Shay. "Your hair is blue."

"That's all you have to say?" Shay asked.

Jacy was searching the drawers and cabinets for weapons or anything that could be used as a weapon. He had a collection of knives so far.

"What's going on out there?" Shay asked.

Hosa shook his head. "The Allegewi has it under control."

"Alone?" Shay's eyes were wide with worry.

"He can handle it." Hosa walked to the wood-burning

stove and took a metal poker from where it was resting against the wall.

"He shouldn't be handling it alone." Shay took the knife from her boot, wishing she could remember the runes carved into Jed's knife. This would have to do. She didn't have time to carve the knife like she'd carved the doorframe.

A deafening roar echoed from outside the cabin. Everyone stilled.

"What was that?" Shay asked.

"My guess," Hosa said. "Is that big Demon guy."

"Alastor?" Shay asked.

"You best friends?" Jacy asked as he tucked the knives into his pockets before arming each fist with the last two, walking toward Shay.

"Never." Shay looked toward the door.

"You can't go out there," Jacy warned.

The cabin shook. The sound of a hundred footsteps echoed from every wall, then the roof. Scurrying and scratching threatened to break through the thin walls.

"What is that?" Shay whispered.

Jacy looked up. "They're on the roof."

Hosa touched the wall, feeling the vibrations. "They're on the walls."

"What are they?" Shay asked.

"Creatures that crawled out of a hole in the ground," Hosa said.

"Demons." Shay looked up at the ceiling as the cabin shuddered. They clustered together for safety. The cabin sounding like it would collapse at any moment.

Suddenly, a pale figure appeared at the door.

"The ghost," Hosa said. "I'll get the salt and make it go away."

"No," Shay stopped him. "She's saying something."

Jennifer's ghost was motioning to the fire in the nearby stove.

Shay shook her head. "We'll burn to death." She rubbed the ring on her finger.

"I will help you," Jennifer mouthed.

Somehow, with the connection to the ring, Shay understood her. "Set fire to the cabin?"

The ghost nodded.

"You'll protect us?"

The ghost nodded.

Jacy touched Shay's arm. "That ghost did not help Jed in the forest. She led him in circles."

Shay watched Jennifer. Communication ran through the ring in unspoken echo of memory. "That's because she didn't know where *here* was. She only knew where these men had brought her children nearby. She said she's never been good with directions."

Jacy made a noise. "Typical."

Shay focused on Jennifer. "She wants us to burn the cabin. It will kill the Demons."

Jacy and Hosa looked at each other. They had nothing to lose, they would die anyway.

The men worked fast, opening the wood burning stove and using the metal shovel leaning against the wall to scoop out the coals. They placed the red-hot embers around the perimeter of the cabin. The old, dry wood of the cabin didn't take long to ignite. Soon, they were surrounded by a ring of fire. Jennifer moved closer to them. She raised her arms and air blew toward the coals, stoking the fire to grow stronger. Flames licked the walls, engulfed the furniture, took over the cabin.

The Demons on the walls screamed as fire ignited them. Shay, Jacy, and Hosa watched as the fire burned holes in the walls of the cabin, then burned the smaller Demons as they swarmed, grasping for pieces of the structure that were intact. Burning bodies fell from the crumbling roof.

Jacy pulled Shay closer.

"That damn thing is going to get us killed," Hosa pointed to Jennifer.

"No," Shay said. "Watch this."

Jennifer opened her arms and her form grew like a lacy sheet. She no longer looked human, or ghostlike, just a swath of filigree that stretched over Shay, Jacy, and Hosa. The cabin burned around them, but they were protected.

The cabin fell away, charred. The bodies of the smaller Demons burned to soot, so devout in their command to get Shay, they didn't stop. Even as they burned, they reached and grasped and clawed until their life-force was gone.

When it was finally done, the three stood on a perch of unburned cabin flooring, and the lacy protective covering floated off them and turned into the form of Jennifer once again. She stared at the trio expectantly.

"What does she want?" Jacy asked.

"These men took her children, killed her and them. She

wanted justice." Shay took the ring off her finger. "Alastor is dead. She got it."

"Burn it," Jacy urged.

"Yes." Shay tossed the ring into the hottest blue flames of the woodstove that was still standing. The metal of the ring sagged, then dripped over the coals as the heat destroyed the ring.

"Thank you," Jennifer mouthed as her ghostly form wavered and thinned and disappeared.

"She's gone to rest now," Jacy said.

CHAPTER 19

Jacy and Hosa took in the scene before them. Jed was battling men who appeared possessed. Shay ran toward him. Jacy and Hosa joined.

Shay noted Jed looked worse for wear. He was bleeding, his clothing was torn. There was a weariness on his face, but he kept going.

Jacy and Hosa weren't far behind Shay. They ran into battle, bodies dropping to the ground as hunting knives sunk into the remaining lesser Demons. Shay tried to get closer to Jed, but the Demons came in waves. Smaller than the others, she could kill them easily, but damn their sharp nails and teeth ripped her clothing and skin.

Jed noticed Shay and her presence gave him renewed energy. He used a spell that tore through the demonic creatures, some set to fire, some froze in place, some crackled and split in half like stone.

Hosa held up a man, his eyes an unnatural black, ready to send his soul to another realm.

"Wait," Jed warned. "He's just possessed. Let me release him."

Jed drew on arcane energy, blue electricity crackled from his fingertips. He chanted words that sounded like crumbling mountains. His fingers twisted into odd shapes.

"What are you doing?" Shay asked.

"Wiping his memories." Jed finally stopped, and the man sagged against Hosa. "He's still a man. He could have another chance."

Hosa shook him and slapped his face until the guy woke, startled and confused.

"Run for the hills, dude." Hosa warned.

The man took in his surroundings. There was no recognition in his eyes before he bolted.

Once the lesser Demons were killed, Jed wiped the memories of the remaining men.

When they returned to the fire, the hole in the ground was closed.

Jed turned to Shay. "Are you okay?" he asked.

"I'm fine." Shay was studying his face. "You came for me."

Jed touched the bruise on her cheek and the crack on her lip. "I'll kill anyone who touches you."

"Don't get too comfortable," Hosa warned as he redirected the others' attention. "We've got more problems."

That was when the dead ambled into the camp. It wasn't

a large horde, but enough that the men backed against Shay to protect her.

Shay pushed at them. "I'm not a child." Jed made room for her to stand with him, knives ready.

"You said they were twenty miles away," Hosa shouted at Jed.

"I haven't watched the news in a few days." Jed's face twisted with forced humor.

"Stupid, Allegewi," Hosa muttered as he swung his hunting knife with focus and lopped off a head.

As the dead infiltrated the camp from the South, an eerie presence entered the North end of the camp. Jed felt it—the change in the air that his mother had taught him to recognize. The hair stood up on the back of his neck as he turned.

"What?" Shay asked as she braced herself for the invading dead.

"There's more," Jed warned. "More Demons are coming."

"Perfect," Jacy muttered before letting out a sharp whistle and a howl. "That was the signal. Iye and Elsu will be on their way."

CHAPTER 20

THE CREATURE THAT WAS CLYBURN STOOD ON THE edge of the camp, focused on Shay. "Out of the eater will come something to eat. And out of the strong will come something sweet." Then Clyburn smiled and held out a dusky hand with long necrotic fingernails and the golden ring missing from his middle finger. He focused on Jed's bag that had fallen on the ground in the center of the four. "My precious."

Jed turned, making eye contact with Clyburn. "You fuck," Jed said as he pointed the rune-covered knife in Clyburn's direction.

Clyburn's eyes snapped to Shay. "Mine."

"Run, Shay," Jed warned.

"No." Shay held her ground. "I am going to rid myself of this disgusting fuck."

Clyburn scraped a toenail into the ground, forming an X. He called his new friends to help.

"Christ, not again." Jed gripped his knife.

"Tell us what's happening," Jacy demanded.

"He's calling more Demons." Jed took a step forward. "This is going to get ugly."

Black smoke erupted from the X Clyburn had made. It twisted and moaned and went to the sky like a columnar cyclone.

Nothing less than chaos erupted. Just as Jacy and Hosa finished with the walking dead, Demons began crawling out of the ground. Clyburn stood to his full height, his arms and knees in the natural position of a man.

The sound of stomping horse's hooves broke through the chaos. Clyburn glanced behind himself before leaping away from the tree line. He ran full-bore toward Shay.

Jed summoned the last of his magic, the sparks from his fingertips sputtering like magic was burning out.

Clyburn was getting closer.

Jed was struggling with his magic.

Just then, three horses blasted out of the forest at the same time. Iye on horseback, bow and arrow drawn. Elsu on horseback, weapon drawn. And...

"Nero!" Shay shouted as the black horse reared up on his hind legs and neighed, sounding like a battle cry.

Clyburn took off, rounding the four near the fire.

The Crow brothers began fighting the Demons that came from the X in the ground.

Jed's fingertips threw sparks that did nothing more than make Clyburn pace in front of him and Shay. Jed noticed

Clyburn's focus kept going to his backpack that was on the ground. He crouched, grabbed the bag, and shoved it at Shay. "Hold this and get ready to run."

Chaos was erupting around them. The Crow men shouted to each other as they fought. Clyburn's lesser Demons were drawing them away from where Shay and Jed stood.

Nero was galloping around the bodies, leaping over some, kicking those that tried to attack him from the back. Jed stepped in front of Shay as Clyburn lurched forward, swiping with his knife and cutting.

Clyburn hissed and stepped to the side. "Out of the strong will come something sweet," he taunted, showing sharp teeth.

Clyburn marked the ground beneath his feet with another X. He crouched, gaining traction on the soil before leaping like a panther. He kicked Jed, one long taloned foot cutting Jed across the chest. Jed went flying, landing hard on the ground. Clyburn grabbed Shay and began dragging her toward the new hole that had opened up.

Behind them, Demons scrambled toward Jed.

"Help!" Shay screamed as Clyburn's nails dug into her arm. She fought and struggled, her heart beating faster than ever as adrenaline surged. She stomped on his feet and kicked, but Clyburn had found a new strength as a Crossroads Demon.

The lesser Demons scampered over Jed as he fought. He heard Shay's scream. Adrenaline coursed through his body, bringing on a new strength. He spoke a spell that sounded like fractured glass as he flicked his fingers. Power blasted around him, sending the lesser Demons into the air, killing them instantly. Jed moved to his feet, energy arcing between his hands.

But he was too late. Clyburn was scrambling down into the hole in the ground, dragging Shay behind him. Jed ran toward the hole, dropped to his knees and slid forward with one hand out. Shay's hand was so close he could almost grab onto it before she disappeared into the ground and the hole closed up.

Jed dug at the ground. He blasted portal spells trying to reopen the hole. He dug harder, faster, his fingers giving off blue energy deeper and deeper into the soil.

Finally, he felt a hand on his shoulder.

"Allegewi," it was Hosa's voice, pained. "She's gone."

Jed turned to see the Crow men covered in gore; panting, sweat dripping down their faces even with the winter chill. Behind them, he saw the glint in Nero's black eye.

Nero stomped, let out a whinny that sounded like a howl, then took off into the dark forest.

Jed gaped at the hole he'd dug in the ground. After all the history he'd read at the Peabody Library and training he'd done with Declan, nothing had prepared him for this... emptiness.

"What do we do now?" Elsu asked.

Jed dropped his hands. Blood leaked from his chest. That familiar feeling returned to him, the one that reminded him not to get involved with humans; don't get involved with women because they all got hurt, they all died. That feeling came back full blast, and Jed hated himself for involving everyone in this mess. It would have been easier to travel alone and stay alone.

Chapter 21

Nero knew where Clyburn was taking Shay. He could sense it now that he teetered on the fringes of the Veil. The mark on his hide burned as the need grew. Nero knew he needed to cross the Veil, no matter how uneasy it made him feel. If he didn't cross now and get to Shay, she'd die.

Memories coursed through Nero's mind. Memories of Shay collecting him in that field, of her tending to the hundreds of bee stings on his skin. She bathed him, tediously dabbed medicine on all the stings. She laboriously fed him from a bottle every few hours. Nero's mother might have left him to die that day, but Shay had saved him and now Nero was going to save Shay, even if it killed him.

Nero galloped in the night, focused on a feeling of darkness in his soul. He was close to a break in the Veil. He could see it ahead of him, an eerie glow resembling ochre candlelight. It was the dark glow of the moon in Hell. The color that the moon on the Earthen plane would soon shine if the thinning Veil wasn't fixed. But that wasn't Nero's problem to solve. He only needed to get to Shay. The rest would be a problem for another day.

———

Sometime between the dragging and the pulling and collapsing into the hole in the ground, Shay lost consciousness. Nothing prepared a human for the sickening feeling of traversing realms.

Shay woke to warmth and the smell of wood smoke. Something didn't feel right. Her body ached, her limbs felt heavy as lead and her eyes felt gritted with sand. She shook her head and tried to move but she couldn't. There was noise; an eerie voice and the sound of crackling fire.

"My precious," a familiar voice hummed.

Shay's eyes flew open. Clyburn had the hand that Jed cut off the Crossroads Demon at the ranch. He ripped open the Ziploc bag and removed the golden ring and bracelet. "My sweet, sweet pretty thing." Clyburn slid the ring on his finger and flexed his hand.

Shay couldn't hold back the squeak of fear that left her throat.

"Ah, you're finally awake." Clyburn moved closer.

Shay lifted her head. She was lying on a table, her arms and legs chained. Her sweatshirt and pants were gone.

Clyburn scraped one long fingernail up her naked side.

"Out of the eater will come something to eat. And out of the strong will come something sweet."

"Get the fuck away from me," Shay spat, struggling against the chains.

A giant figure burst through the door. Wood flew across the room and hooves echoed on the stone floor. Shay could barely believe it was Nero.

"You," Clyburn hissed, grabbed a fire poker from nearby, and ran at the horse.

Nero kicked with his hind legs, hooves connecting with Clyburn's head and launching his body into the nearby fire. There was no life left in the creature.

"Oh my God, good boy!" Shay cried. "Come here. Help me get out."

Nero shivered. It looked like a wave passed over his body. Shay blinked a few times, not understanding what had just happened.

Just like Clyburn took the role of the Crossroads Demon after Jed had killed the original one, Nero now took the role as he had killed Clyburn.

The ring and bracelet materialized on Nero. The ring became an earring in his left ear, the chain dangled down to a loose, golden necklace around his neck.

Shay gasped as it appeared. "Get me out of here," she urged.

Nero moved closer. He gripped the chain around her wrist between his teeth and bit down. The metal shattered and fell to the ground. He repeated with her other arm and ankles until it freed Shay.

Shay sat up and rubbed her wrists. She moved slowly, her body sore and aching. "I need clothes." She wanted to get the heck out of this cave but she didn't want to go naked.

She found a pile of laundry on the floor and dug through it. Thankfully, Clyburn had clothes in his hovel. Shay found a shirt that hung down to her knees. The pants were all too big. She found a pair of rusted scissors and cut them into shorts. Shay rolled the waistband until they'd stay on her hips. She searched the lair until she found Jed's backpack. His notebook and satchels of powders and bones were littered about on the floor. Shay stooped down to collect everything and put it back in the bag. She searched more of the room to make sure she wasn't missing anything before she zipped up the backpack and put it on.

The body in the fire was smoking. The scent of burning flesh was getting stronger. Shay gagged.

Nero shook his head and nodded toward the doorway.

Shay was afraid. Wherever they were, it wasn't what she knew. Beyond that threshold was a land bathed in strange light, strange sounds, and an eerie feeling.

Nero nudged Shay's shoulder, eager to get out of the hovel and away from the burning body.

Shay finally walked, and Nero followed. She exited the threshold and let her eyes adjust. The sun was coming up in the distance, but the land that stretched out before her looked draped in smoke. She rubbed her eyes. "Where are we?" she asked, one hand moving to stroke Nero's inky mane.

———

Nero knew he was running out of time. He could feel the hole in the Veil shrinking as daybreak came. He huffed and nudged Shay but she didn't seem to understand. She was scared, mesmerized, frightened of this dark land. Something broke in Nero's chest. He was different now. More different than ever before. The scratch on his hide had healed with his transformation, but once the life force left Clyburn, it came to Nero. Now he belonged to this land. It was his.

Shay's small, warm hand comforted him and while Nero wanted to stand here forever with his human and feel her warmth and love, he knew she didn't belong here. Nero had to get Shay out.

Nero couldn't speak but he did his best to communicate. He stared at Shay, nudged her, stepped in front of her, offered his flank for her to jump on. He finally noticed she seemed much smaller than ever before and he felt much larger than ever before. Nero searched the ochre land before them until he found a downed tree. He walked to it and waited much like he would wait next to the stepstool on the ranch when Shay was a child. He waited patiently for her to climb up.

"What are you doing, boy?" Shay asked.

The hole in the Veil was closing.

Nero huffed and snorted. He pawed at the stump with his hoof.

"You want me to ride?"

Nero whinnied and showed his teeth.

"Okay." Shay sounded uncertain. She stood up on the stump, jumped and threw a leg over his side. "I don't remember that being so hard," she said, gripping the golden chain around his neck as she got her balance.

Nero began walking at a fast pace, hoping she'd get the message and hold on to his mane. He felt her knees tighten against his sides. His walk transitioned to a trot then a gallop. Shay leaned forward and gripped his mane tight.

He galloped faster. After the scratch he'd been lightning and blood rushed through his ears at a deafening pulse. Now, Nero was light; he was a cosmic ray; he was the expansion of the universe. He was a black hole hurdling through space. Nero felt the crack in the Veil. It was close, but shrinking. Shay made a noise as she gripped him tighter. Nero was worried she'd fall off... she couldn't. She had to hang on. He was running out of time.

There it was, a crack of white light between a boulder and a leafless tree. He couldn't simply walk through it like before. Nero put his head down and leapt through.

CHAPTER 22

Time is a fickle thing when realms are involved. In the time it took Jed to turn desolate on his knees, mourning the loss of Shay and hating himself, Nero had saved Shay and made it back to the Earthen plane. But in the time it took for Nero to get Shay back to the camp where they'd last seen Jed, Jed and the Crow men were gone.

"Oh no," Shay whispered. "We have to find them."

A few men who'd had their memories wiped by Jed remained at the camp. They huddled around the fire, shotguns ready but eyes closed.

Nero didn't give Shay a chance to dismount. He trotted away from the camp, following a path of glowing blue light that was typically left behind by Jed.

Nero knew that this might be the last time he got to spend with Shay. The darkness was calling him; Nero could feel it tugging from his center. He'd have to go back to that place soon, and he wouldn't be able to come back like before.

Another darkness had arrived on the Earthen plane, something with more force, something that Nero knew to fear. It was far away, but he could sense it moving closer–Dark creatures that didn't belong on the Earthen plane were here.

Nero took his time tracking Jed. He reveled in Shay's pats and strokes, wishing he could stay with her forever.

The trail wove away from the nearby road and onto sacred ground. Nero could smell the smoke from a fire. He'd passed two of the Crow men earlier in the night as he chased Clyburn. Now he assumed they were headed back to the camp to plan their next move.

Chapter 23

Jed was dragging his feet. Not only had he lost Shay to a Demon, but he'd also lost his pack with all of his worldly possessions. Everything he'd collected over the decades; fine grains of sand, sacred ash, tufts of hair, gemstones, holy water, and Declan's book. Jed was feeling lost. He'd need to make a new book and try to rewrite it all from memory.

"You'll be okay, Allegewi," Hosa said. The black-haired man reached out and slapped Jed on the back in an effort to comfort him. The force caused fresh blood to leak out of the claw marks on his chest. "Sorry about that."

"It's fine." Jed knew he could heal himself once he'd rested. He'd have to fix the runes that were tattooed across his chest as well.

"Where did Clyburn drag Shay to?" Jacy asked.

"Hell." Jed's head dropped. He'd never transversed realms. He wasn't even sure how to do it. He knew of portals in holy places but none were nearby. Sparrow could help him though; tell him how to get to Hell or even bring him there.

"We have to go get her," Iye said. The Crow brother looked utterly pale and held a hand to his bleeding stomach.

"Brother," Elsu watched Iye, skeptically. "You're hurt."

Iye shook his head. "I'm fine." Blood tinted his lips.

Jacy moved closer, touched Iye's shoulder, and moved his hand away. There was a gaping wound. Iye's intestines were falling out, blood began rushing down his legs. "How are you standing?" Jacy asked his brother.

Iye's face twisted in anguish. Jacy helped him to the ground. Elsu and Hosa moved closer. They scrambled to tend to the gaping wound. Elsu's hands packed his brother's intestines back into place, then he took off his shirt, tore it in half and pressed it to Iye's stomach.

Iye was shaking his head. His entire body began trembling. "You can't fix this." Tears dripped down the sides of his face. "Let me go."

"No," Jacy dropped to his knees and cradled his brother's head in his hands. "No. Don't, Iye," he begged.

"I'll turn soon." Iye held up his left hand that was already turning gray and green. "Don't let me…"

Hosa turned to Jed, "Allegewi, fix him! You have the magic, you healed Shay. Fix him now!"

Jed moved closer, his arms and hands shaking from all the magic he'd used. He knew his aura had to be glowing like the sun.

Iye shook his head. "It's too late." He coughed, turned his head and blood pooled around his lips.

"Do it!" Hosa demanded.

Jed twisted his fingers in and tapped them in mystical dance. He spoke words that sounded like a prayer from a child. Sweat beaded his forehead, his arms shook harder.

"No," Iye whispered. "It's not working."

Hosa grabbed Jed by the shirt and shook him. "Save him!" he demanded, pointing at his brother on the ground.

There was so much blood. Blood pooled around Iye's body and began soaking into the frozen ground.

"I'm trying," Jed shouted back. Jed knew it wouldn't work, but he owed it to the Crow men to try. He owed it to Grandmother Crow for sending her sons to help find Shay. He tried every healing spell he'd ever memorized. Nothing was working.

Iye's body twitched as the living dead curse began taking over his body.

"Don't let me die like this," Iye begged, searching his brother's faces. "Please. Tell mother *neme'hot'tse*." I love you.

Jacy was the one who stopped it. He jabbed his hunting knife into Iye's skull, eyes full of anguish.

"*Neme'hot'tse*, brother," Jacy whispered as the light left Iye's eyes.

Uncomfortable silence followed until the Crow brothers started humming. It was a song deep and mournful, a song handed down from ancient tribes, a song that would guide Iye's soul onward.

Jed stood back and gave them space, his eyes watching the hole, wishing it would open again. It never did.

Jed was tired of watching the people around him die. It

was safer when they didn't know him or when they couldn't remember him. He'd walked across the Earthen plane like a shadow. It was easier when he was the only one running for his life.

Jed kneeled next to an unconscious man, placed his hands on either side of his head, and chanted the spell to erase his memories. When he was done with one, he moved on to another. Only a handful of men were alive. The Demon possession had left their bodies during battle. Jed wiped everything after their possession. They'd wake up not remembering all the evil they'd taken part in. By the time he'd reached the last man, the spell fell from his lips like a kiss; easy, tranquil, final.

———

IYE'S CORPSE was wrapped for burial on the Crow family lands. The brothers would take him home so Grandmother Crow could say goodbye.

Elsu asked Jed about a plan to find Shay as they walked.

"I know someone who can help." Jed scratched his neck. "He should be nearby, closer to the coast. The horde of the dead is following him. I just need to see the news to try to get a better idea of exactly where he is."

"This sounds strange," Hosa said. "What kind of man knows how to get to Hell?"

"He was an Angel," Jed said. "But then he was a Legion commander, part of Hell's policing force. They're called Hellions."

"Why would he be here?" Jacy asked, eyes disbelieving.

"It's a long story." Jed gestured to the sky. "A very long, confusing, fucked up story."

"Seems we've got nothing but time," Elsu said, checking his watch. "Camp is a good thirty minutes away."

The sun was coming up and the air was warming. The figures of the five men cast long shadows in the dappled light that filtered through the canopy.

Jed inhaled a cleansing breath and told them the tale of Meg and Sparrow.

———

THE SUN DROOPED low in the sky, casting a pallor over the frozen landscape as the men trudged wearily back to their camp. None of the Crow men had much to say about the story of Meg and Sparrow, each ruminating on the details and Jed's plan.

Finally, a camp became visible from the trail. There was a squat building within a cluster of trees and shrubbery, barely noticeable to the untrained eye.

Jacy went to get the fire going.

As the embers flickered and the sun continued to rise, the day enveloped them. The camp was a haven, a sanctuary for the weary men who had seen wicked creatures for the first time. The Crow men had heard stories, but nothing had prepared them for the Demons, the dead, and the ghost. It was a culmination of supernatural events that each man needed time to digest. The Crow men busied themselves with chores and cleaning up.

Jed sat by the fire, resting his weary bones and gathering his strength. The claw marks across his chest burned and ached. One brother handed him a bottle of water, another handed him a package of dried meat, then they all sat around the fire.

Despite the fatigue and scars that marked their bodies and souls, a sense of camaraderie and resilience pulsed through the group, a testament to their unyielding spirit in the face of darkness.

"Thanks for not killing me," Jed said to Hosa.

Hosa chuckled. "I never said it was completely out of the question."

Jed took off his torn shirt, using it to soak up the blood dripping down his chest. He whispered a healing spell and held his open palm over the oozing claw marks. Something pinched as the wound closed. Too tired to worry about it, Jed rushed to close his skin. Without his pack and tattoo gun, he'd have to wait to fix his tattoos. Without them, he felt exposed.

"We don't have a television here but we have a radio inside." Jacy said, staring at the flames of the fire. "You might get some information from that."

"Sure," Jed agreed. "Sounds good. Do you have any clothes? I need to go back to the Jeep wreckage and get something to wear later on."

"I'll look." Jacy left the men and went inside the cabin.

Jed drank his water and ate the dried meat. He had a plan. He'd get moving again soon so as not to waste any more time. He'd get to Shay, rescue her, and wipe her memories.

He'd wipe everything. It would be hard to let her go, but Jed knew now that his initial thoughts were right. He's too dangerous. Too many people have died around him. Shay said no once already to wiping her memories but he'd convince her, he might even do it while she was sleeping. Either way, the next time he saw Shay, it would be his last. She deserved better. This was just turning into another Chesapeake City disaster.

"Here, Allegewi." Jacy dropped a shirt in Jed's lap before sitting next to him and turning on a handheld radio.

There was static as Jacy turned the dial, trying to find a station. After a few minutes, he sighed in defeat. "There's nothing," he said.

He passed the radio to Jed, his thumb hitting the dial. A voice rang through clear as day. "Southern and mid-California are complete red zones. Do not enter. The movement is headed north. Evacuation orders are in effect for Del Norte county. Get out. Get out now. The National Guard will not assist. They are headed East as numbers decline." There was a strange noise before static came from the speaker and the channel went dead.

Jed looked up.

Elsu moved to stand. "This is sacred land within Del Norte county. We must go."

The men stood and began packing up. In record time they smudged out the fire and buried the ash, and the cabin was secured for future travelers.

There were four horses for the Crow men. Two had

returned from battle and another two were hidden in a roughly made pen behind the cabin.

"You ride with one of us," Hosa said to Jed. "Or you'll slow us down."

Before Jed could move, the sound of snapping twigs and rustling leaves came from the surrounding forest.

Jed turned, ready to battle once again.

A giant black horse stepped out of the shadows, carrying a woman with blowtorch-blue hair.

CHAPTER 24

"Hey, guys," Shay exclaimed. She'd never been so happy to see familiar faces. She leaned forward and patted Nero's neck. "Look who saved me. My baby Nero came to my rescue."

"That's not Nero," Jed warned. His expression was one of pure horror. "That is not your horse."

"Of course it is." Shay continued to stroke Nero's neck.

"Get off him!" Jed shouted, fear in his eyes. "That's not him."

"It's him. Why are you acting so strange?"

"The creature teeters on the veil," Hosa said. "He is not what he was."

"We wouldn't lie to you, Shay," Jacy said. His eyes imploring.

Shay had known the Crow men her whole life. She knew she needed to trust them. Just what they were saying was so... bizarre.

Shay slid off Nero's back and inspected the horse. He seemed taller–she measured with her palm–by a few hands. She rubbed his coat. It was like polished onyx. She'd never seen it so dark, but figured it resulted from freedom.

"You're the same, right boy?" Shay looked into Nero's large black eyes.

Nero huffed and nodded his head. Shay only saw the abandoned foal she brought home from the prairie that day as a kid and nursed back to life. Nothing more. It was Nero through and through. It would always be just Nero to her because Shay could see nothing else. It was all a mother could ever see, her sweet innocent baby horse.

Shay touched the golden ring in his ear, her finger trailing along the chain and then the chain around his neck.

"That looks like the ring from the hand I cut off the Crossroads Demon," Jed said.

"Nero killed Clyburn. He had the ring on when it happened." Shay shook off the pack and tossed it to Jed. "Clyburn took it out of here."

Jed nodded. He didn't know everything about Demonology, but he knew a balance had to be maintained. He was putting the pieces together. "I'm sorry, Shay." Jed's voice was low. "He's changed."

Shay petted Nero's neck. "Yes. Yes he has."

Nero huffed and pawed at the ground, the tug of Hell becoming almost unbearable.

"Okay, boy." Shay stopped touching him. "It's not a goodbye. I love you."

Nero nodded and turned his head, one large black eye

focusing on Shay before he turned and trotted off into the shadows of the forest.

Shay watched him go. She watched the shine of his coat as he ran through the forest. His image became a blur, and then... he was gone.

Something sank in Shay's heart as she put the pieces together. The speed at which he now moved, the difference in his body, the gold chain. He was more than a mustang released to the wild. Nero was something different.

Shay turned to face Jed and the Crow men. "It's over?" she asked.

"The camp has been rid of Demons," Elsu said.

Shay took note that there were only three of the Crow brothers present. "Where's Iye?"

"Dead," Hosa said. "We couldn't save him."

"What happened?" Tears stung Shay's eyes. A fleeting thought passed through her mind that it was best to die quickly in battle than rot as a walking corpse.

"The Demon battle," Hosa said.

Shay finally noticed the neatly wrapped corpse that was resting beside Hosa's bench seat.

"The horde is still coming this way," Hosa reminded the others.

Shay looked at Jed. She knew if the dead were close, then so was Sparrow.

Hosa and the others were packed and ready to go. "Come with us?"

"We are headed in the opposite direction," Jed said. "He's close."

Shay nodded, knowing. "I'm staying with him." She motioned to Jed.

"Are you sure?" Hosa asked. "There's much danger around the Allegewi."

"I know," Shay nodded as she stepped closer to Jed. "I can hold my own."

The Crow men said goodbye, each hugging Shay as Jed watched with a snarl on his face. He didn't want men touching her.

"Take care," Elsu said as he clucked his tongue and headed back toward Montana.

CHAPTER 25

"Do you want to talk about it?" Jed asked as they walked through the dappled, day-lit forest.

"Not right now." Shay was doing her best to keep up with Jed's long stride.

"Did they hurt you in other ways?" Jed asked, glancing down at her body.

"They tried." Shay wished she had a coat. "I put up a hell of a fight. They didn't get anywhere."

Jed nodded, glad that she hadn't been damaged beyond repair by the men at the camp.

They came up on an overturned Jeep Commander on the side of the road. Jed crouched and looked inside.

"All of our gear is still here," Jed said.

"Did you wreck it?" Shay asked, crouching next to Jed. "Did you get hurt?"

"No more than usual," Jed laughed. "Our packs are in there if you want some real clothes."

Shay shivered. "I'd kill to get out of these rags."

Jed and Shay climbed through the broken window.

Shay found the tarp and laid it out, then set everything on it. She unzipped one of the bugout bags and found clean clothes and a jacket. She moved behind the Jeep and changed her clothes, leaving the dirty clothing from Clyburn's hovel in the muddy ditch.

Jed was drinking water and eating jerky when she stepped around the Jeep, ready to go.

They filled their packs with as much as they could carry, then started walking.

"Did you want to go back to Montana?" Jed asked.

"No."

"You're too confident in that answer. There's more danger on this trip," he warned.

"It's okay." Shay nodded, accepting.

Jed stopped in the road. He gripped Shay's shoulder and turned her to face him. He searched her eyes. "The offer still stands." He held up a hand near her head. "I can make the memories go away. I can make you forget all of this ever happened. You can go back to Montana, go live with Grandmother Crow, and be happy."

"I don't want to do that." Shay blinked, disbelief rising in her chest. She'd already told him no once before.

"You should," Jed said. "You'll be safe."

"I like where I am."

Jed's hand traveled up the side of her neck and he held her cheek. "You almost died."

"I feel quite alive." She leaned into his touch, wishing it

would never end. She wanted to feel his hands forever touching her.

"I will never forgive myself if you die. If you'd died back there with Alastor."

Shay held her fingers up to Jed's lips. "I'm fine. I won't die."

"Just let me make you forget." There was something in Jed's voice, a deep longing for pain, regret, fear. It was all bubbling up inside of him. "Let me erase the memories."

Shay slapped Jed's hands and moved away from him. "I said no. That's what I meant. Stop asking." Shay was getting annoyed.

"Why?"

"I need to remember. It makes me who I am. Without those memories, I will be nothing. I will forget everything. I will forget my life. I will forget what makes me, me. I will forget... you." Shay's eyes were watery with tears. She took a deep breath and wiped at her face. "And if I happen to remember anything about you, it will never be like this." Her fingers were tingling with emotion and although Shay didn't hold magic in her bones, she worried that electricity just might shoot out of her fingertips and damn him for even recommending the idea.

"I'm going to do it," Jed promised. "One day you're going to see it my way. You're going to want out of this mess I've dragged you into. You're going to beg to be rid of me and everything I've exposed you to."

"I will break every single one of your magical fingers if you ever try," Shay promised.

Chapter 26

They had walked for hours in silence. Shay replayed Jed's threat repeatedly in her head. And she wondered if maybe the Crow family was correct in their assumptions about him. He was dangerous. He brought trouble. But he'd also saved her when he didn't have to. He could have left them back in Colstrip, he didn't need to follow them back to the ranch. He could have fled instead of protecting Shay.

She thought about the way he'd cared for her after Nicholas died. He checked her for bites, cleaned her, held her while she slept. Shay knew those weren't the actions of a man who didn't care.

There was a Jeep Wrangler on the side of the road up ahead. Jed pointed to it.

The vehicle was empty, the door ajar as though someone jumped out and took off running. Or maybe they were dragged out.

Shay looked under the hood. Everything appeared intact. She'd learned enough about engines on the ranch not to need a mechanic for most things.

Jed found a key in the ignition and tried to start it. The engine rumbled, then stopped. He tried a few more times.

"Let me try." Shay got in the driver's seat and turned the key. She got the same result. She checked all the knobs and dials before noticing the headlights had been left on. "It's probably the battery." Shay got out and looked around. "We can't jump it without electricity." She secured her pack.

Jed held up his hand. Blue sparks danced. "Lucky me."

Jed opened the hood of the Jeep. Shay turned over the engine as he zapped the battery. The Jeep roared to life.

"I need to use the bathroom." Shay set her bag on the backseat. "I'll be right back." She headed for the tree line, and privacy behind the forest shrubbery.

"There are more camps around here," Jed warned. "Be quick."

Shay nodded. She needed a few moments away from Jed to collect her thoughts. Her foot hit something hard, and she bent to find a solid baseball bat. She took it with her.

Movement caught her attention. Shay walked closer, not wanting a surprise. She'd had enough surprises these past few days.

———

"There was a man in the woods, just down there," Shay pointed to where the road split north.

Jed's shoulders dropped in frustration. "Can you stay out of trouble for one second?"

"He was watching a bird. There was something... dark and strange about him."

Jed stopped what he was doing and faced Shay. "Did he have tattoos?" He motioned to his arms. "Runes like these?"

"Yeah."

"Jesus Christ." Jed rubbed his face and ran his hands into his hair, tugging. "That was probably Sparrow."

Shay smiled. "Oh. I found him then." She pointed to the road. "He's headed that way."

They got in the Jeep and drove in the direction Shay had pointed. All signs led to Crescent City.

Chapter 27

The small clapboard house had been empty for long enough that a layer of dust had settled on every flat surface.

"This town was probably really charming before." Shay looked at the paintings on the wall. "Sad. I always liked coastal towns like this. They're always the setting for a romance movie." Shay shivered. "It's cold."

Jed had lit the stove and was boiling a pot of water. "Hot meal tonight."

"Turn on the oven and warm this place up," Shay suggested, walking closer to the heat, hoping to warm her numb fingertips.

"We should secure the doors." Jed picked up a chair and moved toward the back door they'd broken in through. "This will buy us some time," he said, propping the back of the chair underneath the handle.

Shay locked the front doors and pushed a heavy lounge chair across the hardwood floors. There was a noise from upstairs. The creaking of wood against wood.

Shay turned and ran into Jed, who was already on the move to investigate. The climb up the stairs was noisy. The old house creaked with every step. They took a left, avoiding the attic access, and searched the first two bedrooms, then the bathroom. The noise came again, like scratching on fabric. There was one last door that was cracked open. Jed pushed it with the toe of his boot and flicked on the light switch. An orange cat was stretching against the bedding, claws scratching at the comforter. It looked startled, then bored, before curling into a ball and falling asleep on the bed.

"It's just a cat," Jed said, relieved.

"Good. I can deal with cats." Shay began walking down the hallway.

"They're not innocent creatures," Jed warned.

"What do you mean?"

"They're half in, half out. Definitely touched by darkness. You can't tell?"

"Not on my radar." Shay began walking down the stairs.

Jed followed and by the time they got back to the kitchen, the water was boiling and the kitchen was toasty warm from the oven running.

Shay opened her bag. "What will it be tonight? Beef stroganoff, cheesy mac, or spaghetti in meat sauce?"

"Stroganoff." Jed made a face when he said it. They hadn't come across fresh food in a while. While the camp food filled his stomach, he preferred something more.

Although there were plenty of days that he'd gone without a hot meal, Jed tried to be thankful for what they had amid the devastation.

"I'm taking the cheesy mac. I'd kill for some real macaroni and cheese." Shay tore open the packages and poured boiling water into them. "Real macaroni and cheese. My mom used to shred three cheeses and melt them together. I'd starve myself all day so I could gorge on it." Shay frowned, watching the camp food congeal as it cooked. "What I wouldn't give for a bowl of momma's mac and cheese."

"That sounds tasty." Jed opened the kitchen drawers until he found silverware.

Shay sat at the small dinette table, her foot kicked against a box. She leaned to the side and found a case of Diet Coke under the table. "Perfect." She dragged the case out and offered one to Jed. "They'd taste better cold."

Jed shrugged. "I've learned to lower my standards."

"Hopefully not too much." Shay stirred her meal.

Jed didn't reply. He simply ate and glanced out the window. "The dead should be here soon."

They'd been tracking the horde with the emergency radio in Shay's pack. News reports were inconsistent, but they'd gained enough information to expect the horde in Crescent City within the next forty-eight hours.

"You want to leave tonight?" Shay asked between bites.

"If Sparrow keeps up his current momentum, he'll be headed out of town by morning. My only worry is, he looked hungry and there's a bar down the street filled with people."

"Should we warn them?" Shay asked.

Jed shook his head. "We shouldn't go to places that will put you in danger. We can't save everyone."

Shay stopped eating, suddenly feeling empty inside. Every step of the way here, Jed brought up danger and keeping Shay safe. She was tired of hearing it. Shay wasn't as fragile as Jed kept mentioning. She'd killed an Angel and save his life. She battled the Demons at that camp. One of these days, she was going to have to remind him.

"I don't know how Sparrow is going to react to you. We can't get too close," Jed warned.

———

The master bedroom of the small house was equally small but had street-facing windows. Jed and Shay brought their belongings upstairs and prepared for the night.

"Keep the lights off," Jed said. "We don't want anyone from the street seeing us."

Shay sat near the window, the full moon illuminating the space. "What's the plan after we get close to him?" Shay asked.

"We have to get him to a portal and take him back to Hell." Jed pulled out a pot of paint and a paintbrush.

"What's that?" Shay asked, leaning against the bookcases at her back.

"You didn't want the tattoos, so I have another idea." He shook the pot. "It's paint."

"Oh," Shay glanced at his hands, then shifted in her seat. "You're going to paint me?"

"I'll paint the runes on you, try to protect you from Sparrow. I don't want him to see you as a threat or a meal." He rotated the pot. "This is like henna. It will stain your skin and last a few weeks."

"What if it doesn't work?" Shay asked.

"It should work." He twisted the lid, and it popped. He dipped the paintbrush into the pot and sat next to Shay. "Want me to do your back or your front first?"

Shay swallowed hard. She'd been with Jed for weeks now, but he hadn't made a move since kissing her on the side of the road after they'd left the ranch. Shay would have welcomed him to make a move. She craved his warmth, his touch, his attention. "Maybe start with my back," Shay suggested.

"Turn around," Jed said. "You'll have to take off your shirt."

Shay turned, her back facing him, and she pulled off her shirt, holding it close to her stomach.

He started at the nape of her neck. The paint was cold and tickled, but his brushstrokes were soothing. As he drew the runes to keep her safe, she closed her eyes and imagined in her mind what he drew. She knew some triangles and circles with lines. She wanted to know more because while she didn't have magic in her bones, she could draw and write.

Cool wetness tickled her shoulders, then ribs, then the small of her back.

"Okay, time for the front," Jed said.

There was something in his voice, but Shay tried not to

focus on it. She turned and held the wadded-up shirt over her breasts.

Jed sucked in a breath and refused to meet her eyes. "You'll have to lean back a little."

Shay straddled the bench and leaned against the bookshelves behind her.

Jed moved the curtains to let in more light, then dipped his brush in the paint. He reached for the clothing that she was covering her breasts with. "Can you pull this up?"

Shay pulled the shirt away, dropping it on the floor, and used her arm to cover her nipples.

Jed cleared his throat and touched the paintbrush to the sensitive skin just under her breasts. Each stroke was cold and tickled and was highly sensual. Shay arched her back when the paintbrush touched the underside of her breast. She closed her eyes as Jed painted across her chest to the other side. He repeated the markings, the strokes, the... Shay bit her lip, holding in a moan. Never did she think being painted would ignite a fire deep in her belly.

The paint brush strokes moved down the center of her abdomen, around her bellybutton, then up her sides. Shay could feel the flush in her cheeks as he worked. She couldn't stop the heat that bloomed up her neck.

Finally, the paintbrush paused.

"I have to do between," Jed said, his voice sounding strange, pained almost.

Shay nodded, moved her arm away and covered her breasts with each hand.

Jed trailed the wet paintbrush up the sensitive skin,

drawing the runes, then across her upper chest. Shay wished it was his mouth leaving wet marks on her skin, his tongue tasting her like no one else ever had. She wished... She wished. Shay lifted her chin. She was breathing fast, anticipating. She wanted more than some erotic body painting with Jed.

Jed painted her shoulders and upper arms. He collected her hair with his free hand, moving it away to expose the length of her neck, and painted a rune from her collarbone to just under the sensitive skin below her earlobe.

A soft moan escaped Shay's lips, released from her throat before she knew it was there.

"Are you okay?" Jed asked.

Shay finally opened her eyes and focused on the handsome man in front of her. The muscles of his arms and neck were tense. Jed's expression was pained, like he was holding in a dark spell or curse.

"What?" Shay asked.

Jed just stared, his eyes roving over her. "Have you seen yourself?" He finally whispered. "Are you sure you're just human?"

Shay supposed she looked a certain way in this position, back arched, breathing heavily. She felt her nipples pebble under the palms of her hands. It totally turned her on.

Suddenly, the paint and brush dropped to the floor as Jed moved forward. Both of his hands gripped Shay's head and delved into her hair as he pulled her forward, bringing her lips to meet his mouth.

Jed's fingers tugged, tilting her to his demanding mouth. He kissed her hard, tongue and lips dancing with Shay's.

It had been too long. Too many days of pent-up tension, too many days of adrenaline running on high with no release. Too many near-death experiences. Shay wanted to feel something more than the end of the world and a constant threat. She wanted to feel alive; she wanted to feel hope.

Shay's hands twisted in Jed's shirt, tugging and pulling until she could feel his warm skin beneath her fingertips. Her heart was beating a mile a minute and heat flushed her entire body. She felt like she was on fire, and Jed was the only person who could extinguish the burn. Her fingers slid over lean muscle and the outline of ribs, scars that she'd seen and wished she could heal. Jed tugged her closer. His hands roved down her back, under her thighs and lifted her onto his lap. Shay pressed her body to Jed's, her hands tangling in his shirt and tugging it up and over his head.

Jed groaned as she pressed her naked breasts to his chest. Skin on skin was like nothing else. Velvet and softness and warmth.

There was a noise in the street below.

Jed twisted to hide Shay and pulled the curtain until it was mostly closed, but they could see outside through a small partition. A man was walking down the middle of the street.

"That's him," Jed warned.

They watched from the window as Sparrow walked slowly down the middle of the road, headed for the bar on the corner.

"Do we stop him?" Shay asked, shivering against Jed's shoulder. There was something about Sparrow. He was becoming darker. Shadows slithered from under his feet. Ice crystals chilled the edges of the window.

"There is no way to stop him," Jed warned.

Chapter 28

— — —

The door to the bar was broken and a large, a bloody handprint stained the glossy wood. Jed and Shay sat in the Jeep Wrangler, an unease passing through the vehicle as they realized what had happened last night.

"Should we go inside and see if anyone survived?" Shay asked.

"No," Jed said.

There were vehicles on the streets; the last of the stragglers headed out of town.

"I've got a bad feeling," Shay said as she shifted the Jeep Wrangler into drive.

A vehicle lingered behind. Sparrow moved to the other lane and slowed. A Jeep Wrangler, with the top off, turned in front of him and stopped.

Sparrow grabbed his blade, holding it out at arm's length.

He was met with the rounded end of a baseball bat. He looked past it and recognized the woman from the forest with blue hair.

"You going to slice me up with that?" she asked.

"If I need to," Sparrow replied. "You going to bludgeon me with that?" he nodded toward the bat.

"If I need to," she replied with a smirk. "You want a ride?"

Sparrow looked past her and recognized Jed from the diner in the passenger seat.

"I like to walk." Sparrow secured his blade.

"There's blood on you." She motioned to his hand and face.

Sparrow wiped at his mouth with an open palm. "Got in a fight."

Her eyes narrowed, and Jed whispered something. "I bet you won. Seem the type."

Sparrow smiled; it was arrogant and dark. "I always do."

Something fell out of the sky and landed at Sparrow's feet with a thud.

"What the heck?" the blue-haired woman made a face.

Sparrow bent and picked up the dead bird. "It's a raven." Sparrow stroked the feathers. His fingers petted the thick flight feathers at the base of its wings. He gripped two and tugged hard, pulling them out. He tucked them in his pocket before gently setting down the carcass off the side of the road. He dug a small hole in the dirt with his hands and buried the creature. The eerie sound of a dozen crows cawing from the power lines filled the night.

"I'd get a move on. The dead are following." The chick in

the Jeep pressed down on the gas pedal and began driving away.

"They always do," Sparrow said as he stood and looked up. There were more dead ravens, more feathers went into his pockets–some he didn't have the urgency to bury.

An unkindness of ravens above him cawed louder.

SHAY DROVE SLOWLY down Redwood Highway so she could see Sparrow in the rearview mirror. Cars were passing her as the last residents fled Crescent City.

"He's not right," Jed warned.

"Clearly." Shay gripped the steering wheel.

"We just have to guide him to a portal."

"And where is the closest portal?" Shay asked.

Jed rubbed his face. "I'm not familiar with this area. I know of some back toward New York."

Shay gaped at Jed. "That's on the other side of the country."

"Yeah."

"We have to get him all the way over there. Him. That giant walking shadow who talks to birds?"

Jed leaned back in his seat. "It sounds impossible. But we've lived through worse."

CHAPTER 29

Shay waited at the exit to Elk Valley Cross Road. She turned off the Jeep to save gas and propped her feet up on the dashboard.

"He walks pretty fast," Jed said, digging in his backpack for something to eat.

"Then we shouldn't have to wait long." Shay shivered. She didn't like to be a sitting duck on the highway. The only solace was that Sparrow would be there soon, and he'd scare away anything threatening.

"Why didn't you just ask him to ride?" Shay asked Jed.

Jed chuckled. "Not so sure I want to be sitting in the same vehicle as him. Last time I was in the same room as Sparrow, his girlfriend nearly killed me. I have little trust for creatures of Heaven and Hell combined."

Shay nodded. "Understandable."

A few of the dead ambled by. Shay and Jed held their breath and sat still as stone until they passed.

"I haven't seen them move ahead of Sparrow before," Shay whispered.

Jed nodded in agreement. "There must be something going on up ahead drawing them."

It was just a few hours until Sparrow caught up with them. Shay rolled down the window as he headed toward the exit to Elk Valley Cross Road. "Where you headed, Sparrow?" Jed asked.

He didn't answer. Shay followed, her foot barely pressing the gas pedal.

They followed him past Sunset High School and turned right on Lake Earl Drive. They passed a pub and a T-shirt shop before Sparrow turned left onto Buzzini Road.

Shay and Jed saw what drew Sparrow. There was a giant house in front of them, set on a lake and surrounded by a stone wall. Music thumped from inside.

Shay and Jed made eye contact. They'd seen what he did to the bar in Crescent City.

"We have to shut this down," Shay said. "He's going to kill those people."

Jed shook his head and made a face. "We aren't the police. What those people are doing is a death sentence."

Shay kept driving, looking for a parking spot that was both hidden and close. "They're probably just stupid kids." She thumbed to the road behind them. "Did you see the high school we passed?"

Jed leaned forward to open his bag and take out weapons. "Just so you are aware, I am not a fan of this."

Shay found a spot under the canopy of a large tree and

near the stone wall that surrounded the mansion. They could get in and out easily and avoid most of the zombies that were currently knocking on the gate.

Shay and Jed intercepted Sparrow as he was crossing the front yard and headed toward the door.

"Hey, Sparrow," Jed waved. "I don't think this is a good idea, man."

Sparrow's face was placid, like he couldn't care less. He leaned to the side to get a good look at the blue-haired girl standing behind Jed.

"Sparrow," Jed's voice was demanding. "Look. At. Me."

Sparrow focused on Jed. "I know you."

"Yes."

Sparrow made a noise that sounded like a growl. "Move."

Jed stepped aside. "Don't go in there. Please, Sparrow. We need to get you to a portal. We need to get you back where you belong."

"I'm going in here." His eyes flashed black. "I belong here."

"Don't." Jed motioned to the Jeep. "Come with us. We'll go for a ride. We'll bring you back to Hell. We'll bring you back to Meg."

"Who is Meg?" Sparrow asked, tipping his head to the side in a very birdlike mannerism.

"Meg is..." Jed was at a loss for words. He wasn't sure what Meg actually was right now or how to describe their relationship. "Meg is yours. Meg is your home."

Sparrow blinked, considering. "I have no home." He moved around Jed and headed toward the house.

The music pulsing wasn't much different from the pulsing of blood through veins.

Sparrow touched the doorhandle and let himself in.

Jed turned to Shay. "Do you like parties?"

Shay glanced to the living dead who were pushing against the gate at the end of the driveway. "Not really."

Jed took her hand and his fingers twitched with a protection spell. "Don't get bit," he warned.

———

JED LED Shay into the house and closed the door behind them. The music was loud and inebriated teenagers lingered in clusters.

No one cared they were there. No one greeted them, no one asked who they were. Jed assumed the party goers had given their last fuck some time ago and were now simply embracing the chaos that came with the apocalypse.

Shay pointed down a hallway. There was a room in the back where people were dancing. Sparrow's tall form was easy to spot. They'd found him. Relief spread and Jed and Shay relaxed a bit, no longer carrying the tension of searching for Sparrow.

Jed followed, leading Shay behind him with his hand holding her wrist.

The music was loud; the song was something old with a great beat. Shay couldn't help herself. They could let their guard down for five minutes. Between the beat and the energy in the room, it was hypnotic. She danced as they walked. Jed paused as Shay raised her arms and began dancing with her arms in the air. She shook her head. Blue hair floated around her face as she spun.

A possessive force overtook Jed when he saw nearby guys looking at Shay. One dared to move closer to her, a smile on his face. A glare and a threatening gesture from Jed made the guy move on elsewhere.

Amidst the pulsating rhythm of music and flickering lights, Jed swayed together with Shay on the makeshift dance floor. Their movements were laden with unspoken tension–a mixture of longing and the unresolved tension from last night hung between them.

Shay's eyes were shimmering with uncertainty as she met Jed's gaze, tinged with a hint of sorrow. The music wrapped around them, its melody a haunting backdrop to the unspoken emotions that tangled their relationship. Shay moved closer, into Jed's arms. She tried to ignore the tangible ache in the air–she was left unsatisfied after the painting session last night as Jed made excuses to send her to bed alone while he kept watch. Shay had fallen asleep watching him gaze out the bedroom window, backlit by moonlight, the runes like dark shadows on his pale skin. She had wanted him to hold her like that last night at the ranch. His arm tucked tightly around her middle, his body curled around hers. That's what Shay wanted.

Their bodies moved effortlessly, following the rhythm, yet their hearts carried the weight of untold stories and unexpressed feelings.

Jed's fingers skimmed her arm, then her hip, sending

shivers down her spine. Shay's breath hitched, a fleeting vulnerability betraying the façade she had crafted that morning. She searched Jed's eyes, hoping to find solace or perhaps a glimpse of the answers she sought. She found nothing within the depth of his gaze. So much had gone unspoken between them. He'd tried to wipe her memories, threatened that he would do it in the future. It broke Shay's heart that she was so easy to get rid of. She had nothing left.

Jed, his touch tender yet laden with the weight of unspoken apologies, tightened his embrace, drawing Shay closer as if trying to convey a thousand unspoken sentiments through their bodies moving.

Suddenly, Jed tugged her close so that the length of their bodies were touching. His breath tickled her ear as he said, "Something else is here." His hand pressed against her back. His posture curled toward her as he led her backward, toward where they came. "Whatever is here, it's not human. I have to hide you."

"I can handle myself," Shay said, her body going rigid. She tried to push back against Jed, her palms moving to his chest, but he simply wrapped his arm tighter across her back and lifted her off her feet. Sometimes she forgot how much bigger and stronger he was than her.

"Please, Shay," he begged. "Don't fight me." His eyes were pained as he searched her face. It truly looked like he was unnerved.

Shay didn't like it one bit. But before she could argue with him, a scream rang out and all hell broke loose.

The bodies on the dancefloor were fighting, biting, the

kids were turning. It happened fast. A flood of bodies were forcing their way down the hallway that Jed and Shay were in.

"Upstairs," Jed said as he set Shay on her feet and shoved her.

Shay ran, grabbed the baluster, and went up the stairs two at a time. Jed was close behind her. The screaming and growling became louder.

Chapter 30

Jed and Shay locked themselves in the front bedroom. They watched the horror unfold in the side yard.

"Who is that?" Shay asked, pointing to a dark-haired woman with tattoos.

"That's Meg," Jed said.

"The same Meg who bit your neck?"

Jed's face turned to stone. "Yeah."

"And that one with the short blonde hair?"

Jed shook his head. "I don't know her, but she looks like an Angel."

"And that's Sparrow?"

"Yeah." Jed paced the room. "We need to get to them." He moved a dresser in front of the door, then returned to the window.

"Why didn't they come after you?" Shay asked.

"I'm assuming they had bigger fish to fry."

"Oh my god." Shay's hands flew to her mouth. "Jed… What the fuck is happening out there?"

The scene turned brutal. Meg cut off the blonde woman's arm. There was blood dripping down the stone wall they were perched on. Meg and the blonde woman were shouting at each other. But then, the dead started moving fast. Faster than they've ever moved before. No longer were they dragging their feet at the pace of a lame bovine.

"They're drinking her blood," Shay said. "Look."

The scene continued to unfold before their eyes. The dead scrambled to lick the fresh blood off the stone wall. They pushed and shoved each other out of the way.

"This is not good." Jed's voice was concerned.

And then, the three disappeared into thin air.

"Where'd they go?" Shay asked.

"Fuck." Jed slammed his fist into the wall. "Meg can travel almost anywhere like that. She took Sparrow somewhere."

"Where do you think she took him?"

"I have no clue." Jed wracked his brain for a logical answer, but the blood he saw dripping from Sparrow's boot before he *poofed* gave him a terrible feeling.

———

TERRIBLE SOUNDS WERE COMING from outside the bedroom door. The dresser slid an inch across the floor.

"Can you stop them?" Shay asked, her eyes wide as she reached for her pistol.

Jed held his hands out and chanted a spell to reinforce the door. "They aren't Angels or Demons; they're trapped souls. There's only so much I can do." He whispered a spell to block the noise in the room, hoping the dead would get bored and move on. He reinforced the wall parallel to the hallway with a second spell.

"This won't hold much." His eyes searched the room and fell on the closet. "I can make a smaller room more secure." Jed led Shay to the closet and began using spells to reinforce the walls and the door. "We'll just wait them out."

There was a sickening feeling in Shay's stomach: they were trapped. They couldn't outrun the fast dead, and she doubted she had enough bullets to end them all.

There was movement outside the window.

Shay aimed and shot.

Bang!

Jed slammed the door closed. He shoved Shay behind him. Footsteps echoed on the other side.

"What did you shoot at?" Jed asked.

"A shadow."

The closet door slammed inward.

Meg was standing there. Covered in gore. "Jed, nice to see you again," Meg said as she motioned for them to follow her. "Would you like to get the fuck out of here?"

Shay nodded. She knew Meg would bring them to Sparrow, and Sparrow could help Jed. She wasn't going to follow the same fate as her parents. Shay picked up her bag.

Meg held out her hands. "Let's go."

Jed looked at Shay and nodded. They both took one of Meg's out turned hands.

Poof.

Shay's head was spinning when they appeared in a gothic style church.

Jed turned away and puked between the pews. Shay's face turned sour as she held down, bile rising in her throat. Traveling with Meg was fast and violent.

Everyone turned at a strange gurgling sound echoing through the church.

"Sparrow?" Meg asked.

Shay moved closer. Sparrow was hunched over the blonde Angel.

"Oh, my god!" Meg shouted. "Sparrow, no!"

Jed instantly regretted their situation.

"Kill her!" Shay would not die today. She would not take her last breath in this church. She grabbed the gun from the holster on her him. "Kill her before she turns!"

Everyone was so slow. Waiting.

"Who turns?" The blonde Angel asked as she rubbed her face. "What the...?" She finally saw the bite. "No."

"Kill her now." Shay was aiming at the Angel's forehead.

Meg had her hand in front of the barrel of the pistol. "Stop."

"Cut it off. Now, Meg. Cut it off now!" The Angel screamed.

"You'll have no hands," Meg shouted back.

"I don't care. Cut! Now!" The Angel screamed.

Shay watched as Meg gripped a wicked blade. It glowed

faintly. With one quick movement, she cut off the Angel's other hand.

"Wrap it," the Angel told Meg.

Shay glanced at Jed, wishing they'd never come here. She would have rather stuck it out in that closet than deal with this shit show.

Sparrow was moving to his feet. He looked ghastly and unfocused, clumsy.

"Secure him," Meg demanded, tipping her chin at Jed as she bandaged the Angel's bleeding arms. "But don't kill him."

"What are you going to do with a dead man?" Jed asked.

"Whatever the fuck I want," Meg replied.

Shay had an idea. The walking dead were useless without their teeth. She grabbed a spare shirt from her pack and tore it. She jumped onto the pew and tossed a piece of rope from her bag at Jed.

Shay wrapped Sparrow's face as Jed wrestled with the giant man, forcing his arms behind him. It was a struggle. Sparrow still had a dark strength.

"You should have cut his leg off," the blonde Angel said. "You're going to need to help them. I'm going to pass out now."

Meg moved fast to assist Jed and Shay. She grabbed Sparrow's free arm and twisted it. Jed wrapped the rope around Sparrow's wrists.

"Where'd you get that?" Meg asked.

"Bugout bag," Shay said. "Never unprepared. My parents trained me for times like this." Shay wasn't sure why she added that last bit. Meg didn't need to know anything about her, but she felt compelled to release the information.

Shay jumped down from the pew and Meg walked closer, looking her up and down.

Shay knew Meg was something else. She wasn't tall like the Angel or Sparrow or Jed. She looked human at first glance, but an intimidating darkness lingered across her gaze.

Shay could only stare, fighting the urge to turn tail and get the fuck out of there. "What are you?" she finally asked Meg.

Meg became distracted by Jed trying to wrangle Sparrow.

"Just let him go," Shay said. "He can't hurt anyone now. And he can't go far in this church." He was no different from the cattle. Penned.

Meg watched Sparrow wander.

"Hey," Shay was feeling bold. "What are you?" she asked again.

"He didn't tell you?" Meg pointed to Sparrow.

Shay didn't want to reveal that there had been little conversing with Sparrow.

Jed didn't interject, he just watched Meg the entire time, his fingers tense and ready to cast if she so as much threatened Shay.

Shay could see there was something more to Meg and she couldn't control what came out of her mouth next. "You are something." Shay gestured to the space around Meg. "Dark. It's very dark around you. I don't trust you."

Jed elbowed Shay.

Shay lost her focus for a moment. "What? You're just

Meg? Nothing more than Meg?" Shay didn't believe it. Her stomach twisted in Meg's presence, similar to when Clyburn was nearby. No, Shay didn't trust Meg one spec.

"She's much more," Jed warned. The change in Meg had been drastic. The last time he'd seen her she was just coming into her power. Now she was chaos.

"Look." Meg raised her hands in defeat and the tension broke. "Sparrow asked me to get his friends, so here we are. I didn't bring you both here for any other reason." Meg crossed her arms over her chest. "But now I have a busted ass healer Angel and a zombie for a boyfriend." Meg's stomach growled. Loud.

Jed's hand twitched.

"And I'm hungry," Meg said. "So, we need to get the fuck out of dodge before Heaven sends some shitheads down here to screw things up more."

"I knew that getting mixed up with you was going to send me on the run. I told you I can't trust anyone," Jed said. "Not even a girl who can flash between realms and slay the walking dead like she was born and bred to take on the apocalypse single handedly."

"You've said that before," Meg replied.

"I repeated it to remind myself." Jed ran his hands through his hair in frustration. He couldn't look at Shay, didn't want Meg to get the idea that Shay was important to him.

"We need to get out of here," Jed said. "There are too many forbidden creatures in one room."

"I went through a portal that dropped me here," Meg

said. "Look for arches with inscription. I can't get everyone out of here at the same time."

Jed and Shay walked to the opposite end of the church.

"What the fuck kind of mess did we just get into?" Shay asked Jed. She felt sick as she did her best to hold down the terror and tried not to think about how she was the only human in the building. She was definitely out of her league.

"We just stepped in the hugest pile of shit." Jed was nothing but honest. He wanted to send Shay away, but he wasn't sure where exactly they were. He should have never let her leave Montana.

"How is Sparrow going to help you like that?" She glanced behind them at the wandering dead man.

"This has all gone very wrong."

"At least they're not attacking us," Shay said with a half-smile.

Jed rubbed his face. "Let's hope it stays that way. From what I can tell, Meg needs us to help her."

"And?"

"I think we should help her. Keep your enemies close."

Shay swallowed hard. "Okay." She had finally figured out the familiar feeling she had around Meg. It was the same feeling she had when Clyburn had dragged her down to Hell. It permeated off the woman. But there was an underlying sadness.

Jed and Shay searched, finding nothing that resembled a portal. "There's nothing here," he finally told Meg.

Meg made a face. "I have to check on Teari."

They followed.

Shay didn't think cutting off someone's hands outside of a hospital was a good idea, but it seemed to stop the spread of the walking dead.

Shay got one look at the Angel named Teari and took in her pale completion and rapid breathing. "I read about this in a survival first aid book. I think it's shock."

"Oh, yeah?" Meg asked. "Angels can go into shock?"

"Why not? They're just giant supernatural offshoots of humans."

"Ok." Meg touched Teari, brushing hair off her face. "What do we do?"

"Get the heck out of here," Jed said. "I'm sure there's a car here somewhere. The priest would have needed to get groceries and travel."

"But did this priest hit the road when the dead started walking?" Meg asked. "How do we get him in a car?" She motioned to Sparrow.

"Trunk," Shay said in a heartbeat. It was the only logical option. She wasn't sitting next to him.

Meg nodded. "Let's find it."

They searched behind the altar to the elaborate door that led to the priest's chambers. There's a large office. They search.

Shay rummages through drawers and cabinets until she finds a hook on the bookshelf. A set of keys. "Score. A Cadillac." Shay turned, holding up the keys.

"I hope it's got a big trunk space," Meg said.

Jed was familiar with churches, his mother brought him often enough in their travels. She always expected them to be a safe place, but they rarely were. They never got more than a meal and a blanket before their stay turned to shit. He headed toward the door at the back of the office. These places were all laid out the same. He turned down a few hallways until they came to another door that led to the garage.

"How far to the portal?" Jed asked.

"Almost a seven-hour drive," Meg said. "I'm not sure Teari is going to make it that far."

Jed starts the Cadillac. "There's a full tank."

Shay had never felt such joy. "Good, because there are no full gas cans here to top off the tank."

Meg walked to the front of the garage and reached for the garage door. She yanks it up. They are greeted by shuffling feed and groaning.

"Crap!" Shay shouted.

Meg used her blade to cut off a few heads.

Shay used more bullets than she wanted to part with. The car sped up behind them, rolling over the corpses.

"Meet me at the front steps," Jed said before speeding to the end of the street and taking a sharp turn around the block.

"Come on!" Shay slapped Meg's arm and ran inside.

They ran through the back hallways until they reached the altar. Both ran down the steps, headed for Teari.

"Help me lift her," Meg shouted to Shay.

Shay grabbed Teari's legs, and they maneuvered her out of the pew. She was dead weight, completely out of it.

Meg kicked open the front door to the church just as the

Cadillac parked and Jed jumped out. "Come on. Hurry up." He opened the trunk.

"I hope you could fit groceries from a trip to Sam's Club in there. Sparrow's a big guy." Meg's tone was sarcastic.

"He'll fit," Jed said.

Meg climbed in the back seat, dragging Teari in with her. Shay closed the door with a quiet click.

Jed grabbed Shay's arm. "Let's get Sparrow and get out of here."

Shay didn't like the feeling of the church anymore. She wanted out and was grateful that Sparrow was lingering near the front door.

"Let's go, Sparrow," Jed said, as he guided Sparrow outside and down the steps.

"He's cooperating?" Shay asked, surprised.

Jed made eye contact with Shay. "He must still be in there somewhere." Hope swelled in Jed's chest. Maybe they could help him.

"You're going in the trunk, big guy." Jed backed Sparrow against the trunk then pressured him to sit and fall back. They tucked his legs in before slamming the trunk closed.

Jed and Shay got in the front. Jed was driving. He shifted the Cadillac into gear and slammed down the accelerator, eager to get as far away from the church as possible.

"This thing says we're going in the wrong direction," Meg said, holding up a cell phone from the back seat.

"Nah," Jed said. "We're going to avoid the busted down cars and roadblocks. I've been through these parts before. On my way to California."

"You drove to California?" Meg asked.

"There weren't planes flying when the dead started walking everywhere. They shut everything down."

"Sure weren't. Driving was safest and fastest," Shay said.

There was a long silence before Meg asked, "Where did you two meet?"

Jed and Shay glanced at each other. "Nebraska," Shay lied. Shay didn't want to reveal all her secrets.

"You don't have to tell me," Meg said.

———

JED TURNED RIGHT onto interstate 80. He passed two cars moving slowly. There were more broken down on the sides of the road. There were even some of the dead schlepping it down the highway. Jed weaved around them.

"Why'd you choose California?" Meg asked.

Jed cleared his throat. "You know I've been on the run my whole life. Months ago, the news stations were tracking the horde of dead. There were groupings of them all over the U.S. but the biggest one was in California." He cleared his throat again. "It moved strangely, stopping for days at a time before moving up the coast. I've been around long enough to know those things don't move in a coordinated pack like that. They're usually scattered."

"So, I had the thought that they must be following something... or, someone." Jed accelerated past three dead making their way across the highway. "I reached out to some of my contacts and they told me about the rumors of a tall, dark man walking his way up the coast. No one could tell what he was." Jed snapped his fingers and points into the rearview mirror at me. "But I knew. I knew because I never forgot the day you two showed up with Sparrow in that Canadian tuxedo."

"What's a Canadian tuxedo?" Shay asked.

Jed chuckled.

"Think jeans *and* a jean jacket," Meg said.

"Wow," Shay made a face, "impressive. Wish I'd seen it."

"Nothing like it," Jed said as he slowed to pass a family waving us down from their broken-down minivan. "Sorry," he muttered. "No room here."

"Keep going with the California story," Meg says.

Jed cleared his throat. "Once I started putting the pieces together, I headed that way."

"Why seek out Sparrow when you're trying to hide yourself?" Meg asked.

"Who better to hide with than a Hellion?" Jed asks. "I knew no one was finding him and the walking dead were keeping their distance. As far as I was concerned, being close to Sparrow was the safest option on the Earthen plane."

"It was," Shay said. "Most of the dead kept their distance when we got close to him."

"Why have you stuck with me?" Meg asked.

Jed pressed his lips together as he glanced in the rearview mirror again.

"Why?" Meg asked.

"Because you're different than you were last time I saw

you, Meg. You're stronger, darker, quicker. You've lost your spark." He tipped his head. "What happened to you?"

Meg didn't say a word.

"Whatever happened to you," Jed said, "is going to keep me safe. You owe me."

"Shit," Shay blurted out and pointed. "Army men."

Jed pulsed the brakes to slow the Cadillac and moved into the right lane. A row of Humvees blocked the highway. Men in green fatigues loaded with ammo and weapons were stationed at the roadblock.

"What is this?" Meg asks.

"Some kind of checkpoint," Jed said, rolling down his window.

"Just speed through them," Meg said. "We can't stop."

"Nah," Jed said. "They'll shoot us dead." He rolled down all the windows and stopped the car. "A caddy won't win against a Humvee."

Men in fatigues, carrying lots of guns and ammo, surround the car. "Where are you headed?" The one at the driver's side window asked.

"Saratoga Springs," Jed replied.

"We've got injured," a man shouted from near the back window. "Unlock the door," he ordered. "Medic, medic, medic we need you at the on-ramp now," he hollered into his walkie-talkie.

"We have to get her home and get her help," Meg shouted. "Just let us go!"

The locks click. The rear door is opened.

"Weapons, they've got weapons!" a soldier shouted from the other side of the car.

"Everyone has weapons you imbeciles!" Shay shouted. The tension in the vehicle was sky high.

One of the soldiers dragged Meg out of the car by gripping her jacket and pulling her across the seat. Jed's hand snaked across the seat to Shay's and he gave the slightest shake of his head. The fingers of his left hand were raised and ready.

"Don't touch me!" Meg screamed like a cornered animal. "We have to get her home and get her help."

"Why would you wait that long?" the soldier asked.

A whole crew of people showed up and the soldiers slide Teari on to a stretcher.

"What happened to her?" someone asked.

"She was bit." Meg said. "She cut off one hand and then it happened again and she made me cut the other one off."

A medic checked Teari's pulse. "She's going to code soon," he shouts to the others. And then they ran her stretcher toward an ambulance.

"Wait!" Meg shouts. "Don't take her away."

"Let them do their work," one of the soldiers said.

One soldier motioned for Jed to get out of the car. He complied.

There's another soldier standing at the trunk. "What's in here?" he asked.

Jed said, "Weapons for killing the zombies."

"And a little bit of food," Shay added.

"You want to search it?" the soldier standing near the trunk asked the one in charge.

Shay felt a bead of sweat drip down her spine. This entire situation was deep shit.

The one in charge shook his head.

The soldier patted the trunk and pointed toward the ambulance. "You can go wait for your friend while they fix her up."

Jed, Shay, and Meg got inside and Jed drove away, pulling off the Scranton exit and following the signs to the hospital.

"That was close," Shay said.

"What are they going to do to Teari?" Meg asked.

Jed followed the signs for the emergency room and parked near the sidewalk.

"Go check on her," Jed said.

"And what about Sparrow?" Meg asked.

"We'll watch him," Jed said. "We'll be freezing our asses off in this weather while doing it."

Meg got out and ran toward the door.

When Meg didn't come back out, Shay turned to Jed. "What in the actual fuck?"

"I know." Jed's hands tore through his hair. He'd been doing that a lot lately. Shay hadn't seen him this frustrated, not even when they were fighting a horde of Demons. It made Shay nervous. She wasn't sure what to expect from these people, and she got the feeling Jed didn't know either.

———

A THIN LAYER of snow coated the sidewalk by the time Meg started walking back.

"How is she?" Shay asked. She didn't know these people, but she'd watched Teari get both her hands chopped off and live. It was brutal. She couldn't help but have sympathy for her.

Meg shrugged. "No one could tell me."

Thuds came from the trunk.

"They'll help her," Jed said.

"We need to go," Meg urged.

"And leave her here?" Shay asked.

"It's getting dark. We need to get to the portal. I have to get Sparrow to Hell before we're found," Meg said. There was something about the worry in her voice.

Shay glanced at Jed, eager to avoid any more battles.

"So we are leaving her?" Jed asked.

"I'll come back for her," Meg said.

Shay wondered how Meg was at keeping promises. She had heard plenty of people make promises. She'd heard Jed promise to wipe her memories and their tone was the same.

———

JED DROVE AS FAST as he could toward Saratoga Springs. Meg watched out the window, disturbingly quiet. Jed turned onto I-84E, then I-87N. Dark cities surrounded the Newburg and Albany exits. But in the distance there were lights. It seemed some towns still had electricity. It gave Shay hope for recovery after all of this was over. Maybe her world could be saved.

In the early hours of the morning, Jed pulled into the stone driveway of the cemetery and parked the caddy against the wrought-iron fence. Everyone got out and moved to the trunk.

"I hope no one is watching," Shay muttered.

Jed popped the trunk open.

Sparrow stared at the three of them.

"Come on, big guy," Meg said, reaching for his legs.

Getting Sparrow out of the trunk was a challenge.

When he was on his feet, Jed took Shay aside, stopping under an overgrown oak that shaded a handful of tombstones. His hand gripped her wrist, and he stepped close.

"You can go back." He held a hand near her temple. He closed his eyes and sighed. "You can forget all of this and go back and live your life."

Something sank in Shay's chest. Then it burned. Shay slapped his hand away from her face. "No."

Jed's eyes were pleading. "Everyone dies around me." His grip on her wrist tightened. "*Everyone.*"

Shay motioned to Meg. "She lived."

"She is very different."

Shay touched the tiny scars on his neck. "You want me to go away because of her?"

"Never." His expression turned sour.

Shay searched his features. The sharp cheekbones, the days old stubble, and the blue eyes that made Shay wonder if they were the same color as his aura.

"You send me away and what?" Shay searched his face, her eyes falling on his lips. "You can't take all of my memories. The day my parents died... I can't go back not remembering that. And I'll remember that you were there." She jabbed a finger into his chest. "I'll hunt you down. If you ever thought the Angels and Demons were incessant, I'll be worse. I will be your biggest nightmare."

Jed smirked, fire in his eyes. "You think I'd fear you?"

Shay stepped closer until her chest touched his. "You have no idea."

Meg cleared her throat loudly. "Is she coming or are you going to annoy her to death?"

Shay let out a breath of a laugh.

Jed walked toward the arch, leading Shay by the hand.

"She's a big girl, Jed," Meg said. "Let her make her own choices."

Jed looked annoyed. He'd seen enough death in his long lifetime. He didn't want Shay to become another memory.

"To Heaven or Hell?" Jed asked.

"Hell," Meg replied.

He pointed to the words etched into the stone. "This can go to either."

"You can read that?" Meg asks.

He nodded. "You can't?"

"Tell me what they say." Meg pointed to the arch.

"Gradus ad Infernus," Jed said and the space between the arch wavered. "Step to hell. That's it. Easy peasy."

Meg grabbed Sparrow's jacket at the elbow. Shay grabbed his opposite arm, and they led him through. Jed took up the rear, to make sure nothing followed them through.

The travelers stepped into Hell.

Chapter 31

Shay recognized the feeling of Hell as soon as she came through the portal into the open field on the other side. She recognized the ochre light, the dark shadows. Her eyes searched the tree line for Nero, hoping that he was here. He had to be here.

"Where do we go now?" Shay asked, eager to move and find cover.

Meg points in the distance. "You know it as Centralia, PA."

Shay's gut dropped. They had to backtrack. This was a mess. "Are you kidding me? We just came from Pennsylvania." Shay's hands tore through her hair in frustration.

"Seriously. Please tell me you have functioning vehicles down here." Jed looked around expectantly.

"We do," Meg said. "But I didn't leave any nearby."

"You didn't plan very well," Shay blurted out. She wasn't

sure where the boldness was coming from. Maybe it was her trying to make up for being just human.

"Nope," Meg agreed. "Sure didn't. But no worries, someone will find us sooner or later."

Sparrow made a muffled noise from behind the cloth covering the lower half of his face.

Shay noticed Meg's face dropped. "Come on," she urged Sparrow to move.

The travelers walked down the road, their shoes echoing in the darkness. Shay moved closer to Jed, her hand on her pistol, ready.

"Weird," Jed said. "If I didn't know better, I'd say we already traveled these roads today."

"These are different," Meg said. "Do you feel any safer, now that you're in Hell?"

There was a pause. "All I can say is I've never been here before. But those Angels have their ways."

"Not here," Meg said with confidence.

The sound of shuffling feet echoed. Shay knew that sound. She'd heard it enough these past few months. The dead were here.

"Dead walking. They'll keep their distance down here," Meg assured Shay.

The sound intensified. Jed's back went ramrod straight. "Shit," he said, grabbing Shay's arm and tugging her away from the dead man who was currently running toward them.

Meg moved the fastest. Her blade was drawn and glowing as she moved to the middle of the road, walking confidently toward the fast-moving corpse. She raised her blade and chopped off its head. "Haven't had that happen in a long time," Meg said.

"Why are they so fast? Was it their blood?" Shay asked.

Jed stepped toward Meg. "What does that mean?"

"They usually keep their distance here. Maybe it's because there are so many of us." Meg looked at Shay then Sparrow. "Come on, let's keep going."

They walked quieter this time. Slower dead ambling in the forest kept their distance. Shay was relieved.

"Someone is waiting in the road up there," Shay whispered to Jed.

"Noah, where have you been?" Meg asked.

The guy in the road looked up to the night sky and said dreamily, "Birdwatching. You know how we used to do, watching those songbirds all day long. What happened to it all?"

Meg was thoughtfully quiet for a moment before she replied, "We'll get back to it." There was sadness in her voice that everyone could hear.

The guy named Noah took note of Jed and Shay. "Oh! You brought back friends and…" He leaned around Meg, noticing Sparrow. "What the fuck did you do to Sparrow?"

Meg grabbed Noah's arm. "Do not tell Nightingale. Actually, you are not to leave my presence until we figure this out."

Noah laughed. "No soup for you."

Meg's stomach growled. "I'll have to eat something else."

Shay glanced to Jed, not understanding. Jed motioned to

the scars on his neck and Shay realized Meg and Noah were talking about Meg drinking Sparrow's blood.

"But, seriously," Noah said. "Night is going to be pissed. Beyond pissed, actually. You went back to fix things. This ain't fixing things."

"No shit, Sherlock," Meg pointed to Jed. "This is Jed. He's going to help us." She pointed to Shay. "And this is Shay."

"What's Shay going to do?" Noah asked, sizing her up.

"Something," Meg replied with a dull voice.

Something burned in Shay's chest. "Kick some ass," she said, eager to prove her worth to these creatures.

"I like her," Noah whispered to Meg but they could all hear him. "Why aren't we going to *poof* back to the castle? It would be faster than this method of travel."

Shay's stomach felt sick at the mere mentioning of traveling with Meg. She wasn't sure she could hold her stomach if it happened again.

"I can't take everyone at once. And I don't want to leave any of them waiting," Meg said. "Actually, go get the Hellions. Tell them where we are."

Noah's lips curled into a devious smile. "And leave your side?"

"Don't screw with me," Meg warned. "You've done enough of that. Go get the Hellions. They can fly us back."

Noah's eyebrows raised in jest. "Why don't you fly us back, Meg?"

"You little... shit." Meg lurched forward, reaching for Noah's throat but he disappeared into thin air.

Shay was staring, trying to process it all, trying to make it make sense.

"Let's keep walking," Meg said.

"What are Hellions?" Shay asked.

"Giant, scary Demon warriors," Jed replied.

"But you said Sparrow was a Hellion."

"He was. Or is. I'm not sure. Hey, Meg, what the heck is Sparrow these days?" Jed asked.

"Damned if I know," Meg muttered, refusing to look back at them as she walked further, one hand leading Sparrow.

Jed lingered further behind Meg so he and Shay could talk.

"Are you handling this okay?" he asked.

Shay shrugged. "This is all completely messed up. What the heck was Noah?"

"I think he's a ghost of some kind," Jed said. "These people, I don't know a lot about them. I only know Meg and Sparrow." He searched her eyes. "Are you wishing you'd gone home now?"

Shay pressed her lips together, ready to give him an earful but a shadow from the sky caught her eyes. She looked up to see giant winged Demons flying closer. They were dressed like black ops, carrying wicked blades and odd weapons. They had horns and wings like giant bats. They were massive, the size of Sparrow but thick with muscle. And they didn't look friendly.

"Oh my god," Shay shouted, grabbing on to Jed for safety. "What the heck! What are those?"

The biggest one landed near Meg. He had horns curled on each side of his head. His smile dropped as he walked closer to Meg. "You took too long. We were worried."

Meg threw her hands in the air. "How about, great job, Meg? Or, way to go, Meg? Or, look you found Sparrow, just what you needed to do?"

Three more Hellions landed, their boots echoing heavily on the pavement. They seemed relaxed. Shay was on edge. She'd battled Clyburn and Alastor and the small Demons at the camp, but these Hellions were so very different. She wasn't sure anyone could win against them.

Meg introduced Jed and Shay before asking, "Where's Noah?"

"He's at the castle," the Hellion closest to Meg answered. He motioned to the other Hellions. "Chel, you take Shay. Tukka and Klaus take Sparrow."

Shay backed against Jed as she looked at the one named Chel. He was mysterious, quiet, and when he walked toward Shay, it looked like he only moved in the shadows; a skip and a ripple of movement.

Jed's arm snaked around Shay's middle and tugged her closer. His free hand reached out, fingers twisted, tapping, ready to chant.

Chel paused in front of them. "I will not hurt her." He looked down at Shay. "She is nothing but human. But you," he looked to Jed, "you are something else. What are you?"

"Just another mixed-breed abomination." His arm tightened on Shay. "If you hurt her, I will end you."

Chel's face didn't flex with the threat to his life. He

simply held out his arms. "A friend of Sparrow's is a friend of mine. Until proven otherwise. I will fly you to the castle, Shay. That is all."

Shay wanted to be strong. She didn't want to fear the Hellions, but anyone seeing them for the first time would be terrified. Shay's fingers tapped Jed's arm until he released her.

Shay took two steps closer to Chel. "Okay." She raised her chin and tightened the shoulder straps of her pack.

Chel lifted her into his arms. Shay glanced at Jed, thinking she should have hugged him or kissed him. Just in case. But he'd been cold in that aspect for a while now, since that night he painted the runes on her skin and kissed her like she'd never been kissed before. He kept his distance.

"Wrap your arms around my neck," Chel instructed as he flexed his wings wide.

Shay reached up, and the Hellion held her small body closer to his before launching them into the air.

Shay felt dizzy between the movement and the sound of Chel's powerful wings and the distance to the ground.

"Breathe," Chel suggested. "I prefer not to land with you unconscious. Your friend will be quite mad at me if I do."

Shay took a deep breath and closed her eyes for a moment. She tried to set her mind straight, tried to tell herself that she would not be dropped or maimed by the scary Hellion that was flying her. She was about to be in a castle, like a fairytale... or a nightmare.

"Your first time in Hell?" Chel asked.

"You could say that," Shay replied. "I had barely left

home before this year. Never thought my travels would bring me here."

"You've been here before though." Chel looked down at her. "I can smell the brimstone in your hair. It's fading, but still there." His nares flared.

"Well, there was this Crossroads Demon who dragged me underground. I woke up and it felt strange. Too many shadows that moved. I wasn't sure where I was exactly."

"You were on the wrong side of the Veil. It's thinned and there are holes. Creatures have been passing through. Now that Sparrow has returned, it should go back to normal." Chel veered to the left and continued flying.

Shay wanted to look over his shoulder to see if Jed was following, but Chel was too massive to see over.

"Humans don't belong here," Chel warned.

"Are you going to send me away?"

"No," Chel said matter-of-factly. "This is Meg's realm. She will decide. The Hellions follow her lead."

Shay's eyes went wide as she made the connection. "Hell is Meg's realm?" Her mouth suddenly felt like cotton. "That means Meg is, like, Lucifer?"

"That was her grandfather. She killed him. We just call her Meg. It's what she prefers." Chel's motion changed. He shifted his body and his wings and they started descending. He landed in a U-shaped courtyard and set Shay on her feet.

Chel waited, arms crossed, watching her intently.

Shay stepped away from him and observed the courtyard. There was a leafless tree in the center, hard-packed dirt, a building that resembled a mountain. The design was menacing and macabre and absolutely beautiful. She'd seen nothing like it in her life.

"Your friend," Chel broke the silence. "What is he?"

"Half human and half Angel." After the words left her lips, she was unsure if she should have told him. She wasn't a spy or good at lying and didn't know what Jed wanted to reveal about himself.

"That explains it," Chel said. "Does he have the magic in his bones?"

Shay nodded.

Chel made a noise like a growl and his eyes narrowed. "Be cautious of him." He showed a hint of sharp teeth.

Three more Hellions landed; the two with Sparrow then the horned one with Jed.

As soon as Jed's feet were on the ground he made his way to Shay, his eyes searching her body for injury.

"I'm fine," Shay said.

———

Jed and Shay got a crash course on the realm of Hell. Meg ruled. The Hellions followed her lead. Noah was a ghost and Meg's best friend, tethered to her. Clea was her mother—another ghost. Sparrow was her boyfriend. And Skeele was her Hellion Legion Commander. The Angels were not allowed in Hell—except for Meg's father, an Archangel named Gabriel. There were beings called Deacons who helped the newly dead ascend and kept the balance between realms. After a long conversation with Chel, he explained that when humans from the Earthen plane died, they all went to Hell, confused and unknowing. The Deacons would find the newly dead and bring them to their Safe Houses so the souls could repent and ascend to Heaven or stay in Hell. The power of Heaven and Hell was determined by how many souls a realm had. Currently, Meg had the most.

———

JED ASKED FOR SEPARATE ROOMS.

Shay's heart sank. She didn't want to be alone. Chel led them to a suite with two bedrooms. It was fully furnished with a kitchen and bathrooms and a living room, much like a small apartment. The furnishings were modest but nice. Leather furniture and dark patterned wallpaper gave the rooms a gothic feeling. Shay felt safe for the first time since before the dead started walking on the Earthen plane. Safe, but lonely and drained.

"Food will be brought to your room shortly," Chel said. "If you need anything, just ask. Stay out of the shadows and never go below the main floor," he warned. "Clea stocked the closets for you both. It's kind of her thing."

When the door closed, Jed set his pack down and rummaged through it. He pulled out a Sharpie and set to work warding the doors and windows.

"What should I do?" Shay asked, setting her bugout bag on the nearby chair. "I want to help."

"Why don't you go get cleaned up?" Jed suggested. "We've had a rough couple of days."

Shay checked both of the bedrooms and chose the one with an elegant four-poster bed and deep purple linens. She checked the closet and found women's clothing that would fit her, just like Chel said. Seems Meg's realm took good care of guests. Shay's mind wandered to Chel's warning and what could be kept below the main floor. She walked to the adjoining bathroom and tried to dispel the thoughts of torture and cages and scenes from horror movies.

Shay found fluffy towels in the linen closet. She ran the water and began filling the bathtub. Thoughts of bathing in ice-cold streams and dark Demon cabins flooded her mind. This was better. She dragged her hand through the bathwater and adjusted the temperature before standing and undressing.

The runes Jed had painted on her body were fading. She wasn't sure if they'd actually offered her any protection. Sparrow could see her and the other Hellions saw her clear as day. None tried to touch her though. Maybe the realms changed the spells? Shay wasn't sure. She released her pistol from the holster, then took off her belt and set it all on the bathroom counter. The Hellions didn't bat an eye at her carrying weapons, they didn't even check their bags. They must have no fear.

CHAPTER 32

Shay toweled herself dry and checked the runes on her skin in the mirror. They were definitely faded after her bath. She turned to get a view of the ones on her back. They were the same. Shay shivered at the thought of Jed painting her again. The experience was nearly too much. She wasn't sure she could handle being that close with him and then being sent to bed like a child again. Shay dried her hair before wrapping the towel tighter around her body and walking to the bedroom closet.

She searched through the clothing and found a pair of dark denim jeans, a flannel shirt, and undergarments. She hadn't met Clea but she sure appreciated that the ghost could match her style and size. Shay dropped the towel and put on the undergarments. The jeans were form fitting but stretchy. She was buttoning the flannel shirt when she heard a noise behind her.

She turned to find Jed staring at her.

"What?" she asked.

Jed cleared his throat. "Dinner's here." He was staring at her exposed midriff.

Shay buttoned her shirt the rest of the way and followed him.

There were two plates waiting on the dinette table. Each had a large steak, a baked potato, and green beans with a large slab of butter. And... macaroni and cheese in a ramekin. There was a basket of bread and two cans of Coca-Cola dripping with condensation.

"Wow," Shay said as she sat. "I wasn't expecting his."

"I'm going to go wash up before eating," Jed said. "Go ahead and eat. I'll just be a few minutes."

Jed was covered in dust, his clothing stained with gore and fingers stained from the Sharpie.

"That's probably a good idea," Shay agreed. As she sat, he walked into the opposite bedroom.

Shay picked up a fork and knife and cut the steak. She sliced the potato then added butter, and salt and pepper.

It was the best food she'd eaten since living on the ranch. She reached for the ramekin of macaroni and cheese, dug her fork in and took a bite. Memories... of her mother and father, of her anger when they said she couldn't go to college and risk the walking dead, memories of running off to that dive-bar and seducing Clyburn. Her mind spiraled at that point. Everything hit her like a flash bang. The Crossroads Demon attack. The Demons killing her mother. Her father changing into one of the walking dead and attacking her. Leaving Nero.

Tears were streaming down Shay's face as she chewed. So much had changed in such a short period of time. She'd seen things that only existed in books and movies. She'd fought and killed an Angel. She'd survived being kidnapped by Demons. She was free of Clyburn thanks to Nero. Shay mourned all that she'd lost. She mourned her simple life on the ranch, the chance to go to college and be normal, the love of her parents. She mourned losing Nero to whatever darkness he was now. She wasn't sure she'd ever see him again. Jed's cold shoulder made it all worse. One moment he was protective, the next he was distant. It was all too much for her to take.

Shay stood up and paced the room. She wiped her face. The weight of grief pressed upon her like a suffocating blanket. Shay crumbled. Pappa and Momma's deaths were a loss that tore through her heart with merciless claws, leaving her shattered and adrift in a sea of overwhelming emotions.

Tears streamed down her face, sobs wracked her body. Memories of dinners and holidays and summers on the ranch intertwined with the stark reality of her current situation. She was no longer on the Earthen plane. She was in an unfamiliar place with dangerous creatures. She was more alone than she'd ever been in her entire life. She felt hollow and desolate, each memory a reminder of the laughter and love that she'd never experience again.

Jed's bedroom door creaked open, concern etched deeply into his furrowed brow as he took in the heartbreaking sight before him.

With a towel secured around his waist and water dripping down his body, Jed crossed the room. His steps were measured yet filled with urgency, afraid to exacerbate the fragile shell of emotions surrounding Shay.

Shay turned, her face tear-stained, her eyes mirroring a tumultuous sea of emotions; pain, loss, and desperate yearning for solace.

Jed enveloped her in a tender embrace, drops of water soaked into Shay's clothing but she didn't care. She rested her cheek against his bare chest, sobs echoing in the quiet room.

Jed was at a loss. He wanted to reassure Shay that she wasn't alone in navigating the unfathomable depths of their predicament. He was there, he just couldn't find the words. It seemed everything he'd said to her recently came out guarded.

Shay's cries softened into quiet sniffles as she listened to Jed's heartbeat. He held her close, warmth seeping into her bones.

"What's wrong?" he asked.

"It's all gone to shit. Everyone is dead and now we are in Hell." She felt his arms loosen and that was all she needed to fall off the deep end again.

"It's not all shit," Jed said. "We got hot showers and dinner."

Shay smiled but anguish threatened to overcome her once again when he slid his hands to her arms like he was going to move her away.

"You don't want me with you," Shay said, pushing at his bare chest.

"That's not true."

"It is." Shay pushed him away. "I lost everything. *Every-thing*. You are all that I have left in this world and you don't even want me."

Shay paced the room, hugging herself.

"You have more than me." Jed's expression was unreadable.

"Who? Who do I have?"

Jed's gaze searched her face. "You have to have more family on the Earthen plane. You have Grandmother Crow at least. The Crow brothers. Friends. You have others who won't put you in danger like I do."

"You're wrong." Shay walked closer to him. "Everyone is dead. And I do not want to spend the rest of my life on the reservation. I will always be an outsider there. You are all I have Jed. When are you going to realize that?"

Jed was afraid it would come to this. Shay knew what she wanted, she knew who she was and he'd been keeping her at arm's length since he kissed her in Crescent City. The truth was, he couldn't get the image of her painted with runes and half naked in the moonlight out of his head. He thought about it every moment.

Shay was pacing until she finally threw her hands up in the air in silent resignation and started walking toward her bedroom door.

"Wait," Jed reached for her but she kept going.

He caught up to her in a few long strides, grabbed her shirt and turned her to face him.

"You're not alone, Shay-baby." He backed her up against

the wall. "You'll never be alone. I'm sorry if I made you felt that way. It's just... everyone close to me has died—"

"Same here, cowboy."

The corner of his mouth twitched. "I'm sorry."

"It's not your fault."

He was so close Shay rubbed the tip of her nose against his.

"It feels like my fault," he confessed. "It all feels like my fault. Ever since I met you at that casino it's been my fault."

"The world's problems are not because of you." She pressed a hand to his chest, feeling the dips and planes of his body as her hand moved up to his neck. "You didn't start the apocalypse. You didn't make the dead walk on the Earthen plane. You didn't kill my parents."

"Sometimes my world is very small. I've only had one focus and that was to stay alive." He leaned against her, pressing her to the wall with his whole body, caging her between his arms. "Now my only focus is to keep you alive."

"I can handle myself. I killed that Angel before it could kill you," she reminded him.

Jed nodded, remembering. "I wish I'd seen it."

"Maybe that's why you can't seem to remember because you were unconscious. I didn't die then." Shay licked her lips. "I'm stronger than you think. But..."

Jed searched her eyes.

"I cannot continue on like this," Shay confessed. "I need you to decide what we are together. I can't go on feeling alone. It's too much."

"You're not alone." Jed's hands touched the sides of her face and his fingers slid into her hair. "You'll never be alone."

"Stop trying to push me away," she begged.

Jed's lips pressed to Shay's. He kissed her, hungry and possessive. His fingers twisted in her hair, his thumbs pressed against the hollows under her jaw before sliding down her throat.

The floodgates opened again as he kissed her like a man starved, like she was oxygen and he needed her to breathe. Shay couldn't stop her tears from sliding along his fingers and down his arms.

"I'm sorry," Jed whispered against his lips. "If I made you think I didn't want you. I've always wanted you since the moment I saw you at Lame Deer Casino. I never stopped wanting you." His tongue speared into her mouth and he nibbled at her lips. He pulled his arms away from the wall and his fingers went to the buttons on her shirt. "I wanted you so badly the night I painted the runes on your skin."

Jed tugged at her shirt and the buttons went flying. He leaned back, tracing the fading runes on her abdomen with his fingertips.

Shay shivered at his touch. His hips were still pressing against her body, keeping her secured against the wall.

"This night was my favorite. I think about it every moment." Jed's eyes flashed to hers. "Did you know that?"

Shay was out of breath from his kisses. "You sent me to bed like a child."

"No." He kissed her hard, his hands gripping her waist. "I sent you to bed because I didn't trust myself for one more minute. Is this what you want?" His hands moved across her back, down to her hips and he pressed her against the bulge behind his towel. "Once we do this, I can't stop. You're mine. Forever."

"Yes." Shay gripped his biceps, afraid he'd change his mind the next instant. "Don't leave me alone. Don't make me be down here alone. I can't do it alone."

Jed moved away and Shay instantly felt cold. It lasted only a moment though before he lifted her and kicked open the bedroom door. He crossed the room and set Shay to her feet near the bed. He pushed the flannel shirt off her shoulders and let it drop to the floor. He traced the fading runes and bruises and scratches she'd endured on their journey. He whispered a healing spell over the scratches. Shay watched his lips as he murmured strange words that sounded like a good promise. It made her ears tingle. Her skin felt warm, electrified. When she looked at her arms again, all the scratches were healed.

"Thank you," Shay whispered, touching him. Her fingers glided over the rounded muscle of his shoulders as he kneeled, unbuttoned her jeans, and pulled them down to her ankles. She kicked them away. His fingers tested the elastic of her underwear before he slid a hand under the fabric at her hip and stood. She moved backward, falling on the bed. Jed pulled the scrap of fabric down her legs and tossed them aside.

"Lose the towel," Shay said.

Jed was sculpted like that Angel she'd killed but with a human softness she couldn't describe. He crawled toward her on the bed, supporting his weight with his arms. His mouth touched her thigh, leaving wet kisses that made her shiver as he worked his way up her body. His mouth touched the hollow of her hip, the softness of her stomach, the firm stretch of her bottom rib, the sensitive skin under her breast. Shay was trembling by the time he made it to her mouth, which he devoured. Shay's fingers stretched into Jed's hair as she kissed him back, desperate for his touch. He palmed her breast before his hand roved over her waist and hip to the apex between her thighs.

Shay gasped as he touched her, as his fingers worked her over and made her ready. When he finally slid into her, Shay was aching and burning.

He kissed her and she kissed him, pausing to take slow breaths with their foreheads pressed together as they moved unhurriedly together. Jed was slow. So slow that Shay thought she might burst into flames from the heat of it all.

———

SHAY WOKE to Jed leaning over her, his hands cradling her face, his lips whispering a spell she'd never heard him chant before. Her mind felt fuzzy, her brain hurt. She blinked a few times. There was a sharp pain in the center of her forehead.

Jed's face was intent as he chanted. His fingertips traced invisible shapes above her ears. He whispered words that sounded like the saddest bird song, mournful and low and heartbreaking.

Shay panicked.

He was doing it. He was wiping her memories. No!

CHAPTER 33

S HAY MOVED FAST, WHIPPING HER FIST UP AND cracking Jed on the side of the head. She shoved his upper body while he was stunned, knocked him on his back, and straddled his chest. She grabbed his hands, twisting his fingers until she could feel the resistance of bones and tendons.

"What the fuck do you think you're doing, Jed?" She screamed at him. "Erasing my memories? I told you no. I told you I didn't want that."

"I wasn't erasing them." He stared at her, hard and cold. "I was putting them behind a wall. So they weren't constantly making you sad." Jed bucked up and rolled so Shay was under him. "I was trying to help you."

Shay stilled and searched his eyes in the dim light. Her hand moved to his face and she traced her fingertips over his cheekbones.

"You could have asked." She searched his eyes. "You

could have asked and made sure that was something *I* wanted."

Jed opened his mouth to speak but before he could say anything, a loud crash filled the room as the bedroom door was kicked in.

A giant Hellion ran into the room and tore Jed off Shay.

"Meg demands that no human will be harmed in her Kingdom." Chel glared at Jed. "You're coming with me."

———

IT HAD all happened so fast. One minute she was warm and falling asleep on Jed's chest. Her body was deliciously sore. The next, he was violating her trust then torn from the room.

Shay rubbed her eyes and held the sheet to cover herself.

"Chel?" She shouted as he slammed the door to the suite, dragging Jed along with him.

Shay scrambled out of bed and got dressed. She found her boots and put them on before running out of the room.

She paused in the dark hallway. She didn't know which way they had gone. It was too dark to see. There was a scratching sound from the shadows.

"Chel?" she shouted. "Jed?"

Panic started rising in Shay's chest. She wasn't sure where to go or where to look for them. One thing came to mind: the levels below the main floor.

Yes, that had to be where Chel had taken Jed. Shay ran back into the room, found her bag, and pulled out her pistol and knife. She left the room again, backtracking from the direction Chel had brought them earlier that evening.

Shay's boots made a hollow noise as she ran down the long hallway. She stopped at the winding, grand staircase and looked down the center of it. It never ended and dark echoes came from below.

Shay ran down the steps, two at a time.

She stopped short when a white figure appeared at the landing she was approaching. A woman appeared with dark hair and ruby red lips. She was slightly transparent like Jennifer's ghost but became more solid as Shay slowed.

"Where are you going, child?" the ghost asked.

Shay tried to dodge around the woman, but the ghost was quick and blocked her every move.

"Let me pass," Shay demanded.

"I do not like to ask the same question twice." The woman tipped her head down.

Shay realized she the ghost looked like Meg. It was Clea, her mother.

"I'm going to find Jed." Shay tried to pass again but Clea blocked her.

"You do not want to go down there, human child," Clea warned. "There are things not meant for your sight, things you can't comprehend, things that are ages old and not mean for human eyes."

"I've seen things." Shay backed up five steps. "I'm not afraid."

"Perhaps I am afraid for you," Clea warned.

"I need to get to Jed."

"What did he do to you?" Clea asked. "We all heard you screaming."

"He made me mad."

Clea smirked. "Are you going to save him?"

"Wouldn't be the first time." Shay glanced at the banister and considered leaping across to the other side. Her stomach clenched when she considered the possibility of falling.

As though Clea could read her mind, she stepped to the side. "I warned you." She disappeared up the stairs.

Shay shook her head in disbelief and ran down the stairs toward the dungeon.

CHAPTER 34

During the reign of Lucifer, Demon children were not to be seen and not to be heard. Breaking either rule would result in severe punishment. It felt awful at the time but Chel would learn it was to prepare him for life under Lucifer's thumb. Chel learned early how to hide in the shadows. He learned how to avoid the light. Bred to be a Hellion and serve the throne, he spent his childhood years in training. It was the only thing that made his father proud. The only time he'd heard his father utter a whisper of delight was the day he'd completed his training. There had been no joy in the family household for years prior.

Chel would never forget that day because there should have been four people at the dinner table, but his sister's seat remained empty, as it had for nearly two years since she'd gone missing. It was the first moment in a long time that anyone uttered an emotion besides despair.

Demon women weren't known for their longevity. Many

died in childbirth or defending their young from rage-filled fathers. It was a family dynamic like nothing else. Lucifer's reign kept his subjects in a constant state of dread. It trickled through day-to-day life like a dark tap left to drip and drip and drip.

Yelena was three years younger than Chel. She spent almost all of her time with their mother. Raised to be nothing more than a breed horse, she spent her time learning how to survive childbirth and motherhood. One day she was sent to the nearby stream to collect water for washing laundry and never returned. She was never found and it was assumed that she was murdered. A dark lull hung over Chel's family ever since. And Chel found he harbored an extreme dislike for any man who could harm a female.

———

"WHERE ARE YOU GOING?" Chel stopped Shay on the winding stairwell. His form was intimidating. The Hellion was huge, dressed in battle gear with a blade strapped to his hip.

"Where's Jed?" she demanded.

"Being punished."

"He didn't do anything."

Chel's eyes narrowed. "It sounded like he did plenty."

"You weren't there. You don't know." Shay swiped at a strand of hair and tucked in behind her ear. "It's a misunderstanding."

"What did he do to you?" Chel crossed his arms, waiting for her answer as though he had all the time in the world.

"I thought he broke a promise, but I misunderstood." Shay glanced away, not wanting Chel to see that what Jed did was still hurtful. She didn't want him using spells that would alter her memories.

"What did he do then?

"He tried to bury my memories so they wouldn't make me sad."

Chel's brow furrowed as he glared down at her. "Sounds like bullshit."

"It was."

"Meg gave orders you are not to be harmed by anyone in any manner." He shifted his feet. "You are well?"

"I'm fine."

"So you want me to release him?"

"Yes."

Chel's face shifted to a semi-growl, showing sharp teeth. He didn't believe her. He didn't trust the half-breed. "Go back to your room."

"I'm going with you to get him." Shay stood her ground.

"Go," Chel pointed up the stairs.

"I'll just get him myself." Shay weaved around Chel's enormous frame and began running down the stairwell again. It didn't take long for Chel to catch up to her. He gripped her by both shoulders with giant hands.

"There are things not meant for human eyes," he said.

"I've seen plenty already."

Chel sniffed the air and was reminded of the scent of

brimstone that clung to her hair. "Fine," he said. "But I warned you."

They walked below the main level. The stairwell twisted and twisted. The lights became dimmer. The noises grew louder. Shay's heart beat heavy as she anticipated what she'd be exposed to in the castle's dungeon. Gothic décor turned to stone dripping with moss and stained water rivulets. Chel passed three floors before stopping their descend.

CHAPTER 35

Nero felt the moment Shay crossed the threshold into Hell. He'd been resting inside the Crossroads Demon hovel, deep asleep and recovering from rescuing Shay. The wound on his flank had opened again and throbbed. Black fluid leaked down his leg and Nero wished for a cold Montana stream to soak in. He was sure he could find a stream here but he didn't know what other creatures lingered below the surface. Maybe if he could find Shay she could help him.

Nero lifted his head and shook. The golden chain dangled and tugged at his ear. The gold was nothing more than a manacle that stole his freedom. Nero was a creature of Hell now. His soul was tethered to the realm just like he was tethered to Shay. It was worth taking on to see Clyburn turn to ash in the nearby hearth. Nero could not think of a better ending to that rotten man's life.

Nero moved to stand, his knees and joints aching from

spending too much time on the Earthen plane with Shay. While he'd reveled in spending time with her before they'd found Jed and the Crow men, it took a toll. Nero couldn't spend long lengths of time where he didn't belong any longer.

He left the hovel and followed the tugging in his chest. Shay was in Hell but very far away from him. He headed away from the coast where the hovel was etched into a barren valley. He trotted then galloped, urgency drove him. Remember, Nero was fast. Nero was the fastest thing between the realms. He felt the tether thrum with danger. Shay yelled. It was nothing more than an echo in his ears. She was so far away. So, so far away. Nero tipped his head and ran faster. He was a blur, the darkest shadow, an errant breeze that left behind a cold chill. Nero didn't know who held the throne in Hell. He didn't know that she could travel in a *poof* of a second. He didn't know that he ran nearly as fast as she could travel. He took it as part of his being, embraced it, knew it was a gift that would keep on giving when it came to ensuring Shay's safety. It was all he could do for the human who'd saved him when he was a dying foal.

His hoof prints left an inky seepage from the wound on his flank.

CHAPTER 36

———————

IN THE DEPTHS OF THE ANCIENT DUNGEON, WHERE the air hung heavy with the scent of damp stone and the echoes of distant drips reverberated through the labyrinthine corridors, Jed's cell had no light other than the dull bulb that hung in the hallway. Strange sounds and smells came from nearby. Jed touched the iron bars only to pull his hands back quickly, his fingertips red and singed.

He chanted a spell to release the lock but it didn't work. Sparks sputtered to nothingness on his fingertips. Jed paced the small space, cursing himself for going too far as he searched for runes or charms within the cell that could block his magic. He could still smell Shay's scent lingering on his skin, and it was driving him insane. Jed wanted to know where she was. He didn't trust Meg's Hellions or any crea-ture in this realm. He'd worked too hard staying alive for it all to end like this. Jed was becoming more and more frustrated as the minutes ticked by.

———

Shay followed Chel through the dark hallways that twisted and turned. The doorways were spread far apart, most with iron bars, some with aged wood and small windows. The bare bulbs that were strung across the ceiling every few feet cast flickering shadows on the moss-covered walls, illuminating eerie passageways that seemed to stretch endlessly into darkness. Shay's heart hammered in her chest, driven by the urgency of finding Jed. The chilling atmosphere seemed to whisper tales of forgotten sorrows and lingering curses that haunted the ancient walls.

"Don't look into them," Chel warned, motioning down the hall. "There are creatures who will eat your soul with once glance."

"Why do you keep them here?" Shay asked. A distant humming sound from the hallway they passed was a desperate plea that resonated deep within Shay's soul. She quickened her pace to get away from the haunting echoes that would lead her deeper into the heart of the dungeon.

"They've been here for ages. We will not release them."

"Maybe relocate them," Shay suggested.

"Too risky." Chel made a noise in his throat as he neared a cell with a guard sitting outside of it.

The Hellions nodded. The one sitting in the chair didn't glance at Shay but kept his eyes elsewhere.

Shay knew she wasn't supposed to look in the cell, but Sparrow was standing right there, twitching and jerking as the death overtook his body. His skin had taken on an unnatural coloring of gray and green bruising.

Shay struggled with what she was witnessing as Meg kept Sparrow locked up. If there was a cure for whatever made the dead walk, she wished she'd known before her parents died. She would have rather cured her father than stabbed him in the head. Shay shivered as the memory replayed. She took in a stuttered deep breath and tried to clear her mind. She couldn't go back in time. She couldn't save them. She could only move on.

Chel led her down more hallways, sensing her grief.

"Why are you sad?" Chel asked.

"My parents died recently. A Demon killed my mother, and I killed my father after he turned into one of the walking dead."

Chel stopped walking and turned. "I am sorry for this." The Hellion searched her eyes, and he was silent for so long that Shay looked away. "My sister passed unexpectedly," Chel finally said.

"I'm sorry," Shay said, reaching out to touch his arm in comfort.

A clattering sound echoed in the hallways. Chel's focus snapped to a nearby door. "Keep walking."

The remainder of the walk was in silence.

———

"Here," Chel stood in front of a closed cell door.

Shay looked past the bars to see Jed staring down at his hands, defeated.

"Jed!" Shay ran forward and touched the bars, only to have her hands scorch from the strange iron.

Chel pulled her back. "Don't touch," he warned before inserting a metal key into the wall. The bars of Jed's cell opened.

Shay ran forward, stumbling into Jed's arms.

"I'm sorry," Jed said. "I'm so sorry."

Chel motioned for them to get moving.

"Let's get out of here," Shay said.

———

CHEL WAS EERILY silent as they navigated the maze-like halls of the dungeon. He led them up the winding stairs and back to their suite. Before he closed the door, he focused on Jed. "If I ever hear her scream again, you're dead."

Jed stood his ground and crossed his arms, promising nothing.

The door closed.

Poof.

Meg appeared in the room; bloody, dripping in gore, her eyes wide with dread. She was carrying a baby wrapped in a blood-covered blanket.

"What the heck?" Shay said.

Meg ran across the room and thrust the bundle into Jed's arms. "No time to talk. Protect this kid with everything you've got."

Poof.

Meg was gone.

Shay moved toward Jed, a sickening feeling growing in her stomach. She leaned closer to the baby, taking in its dark hair and blue eyes. "Jed, whose baby is that?"

Jed touched the blood-stained blanket, pulling it away from the baby's face. The child was beautiful, like nothing he'd ever seen. Terror filled Jed.

"Hold this baby, Shay," he passed the child into Shay's arms. "Just... stay right there. Don't move until I'm finished." There was a concern in his voice that she'd never heard before.

Jed ran for his pack, brought it into the living room, and poured it out on the table. He grabbed chalk and sand. "I'm going to need you to stand there for a while." Jed drew a circle around Shay and the baby. He scrambled, drawing runes as fast as he could. He switched to coal eventually, accentuating the chalk, then poured a thick line of sand around the circle.

"What are you doing?" Shay asked. She'd never seen him so frantic. She'd never seen him set to work with the runes and protection spells so quickly. He lit a candle, then a bundle of sage, and left it to smudge in the corner. He etched runes into the doorway, then the wall. The floor became a tapestry of spells and protection charms.

"Do you think all of this is necessary?" Shay asked, her legs feeling tired. The baby was asleep in her arms. "Jed!" Panic was making her body ache.

He finally paused to look at her. "What?"

"What are you doing? Please tell me."

"That," he pointed at the baby, "is an Angel's baby and I have no idea why Meg has it, but we will not be murdered over whatever cluster fuck she's gotten us into."

CHAPTER 37

JED SHOULD HAVE KNOWN THAT DEMONS NEVER DIE once. But all the books on Demonology that he'd studied at the Peabody library never mentioned it. There was still much unknown between the realms. He'd learn, eventually. He'd learn enough to rewrite the books in the Peabody library so that future generations of half-breed humans might have a chance–if they lived long enough to learn how to read.

Alastor was a Demon of Lucifer's time, left to disrupt and damage as he saw fit. He supported his throne by collecting souls and selling them to the highest bidder. Children were worth the most, and he'd created a lucrative human trafficking scheme. Creatures depended on Alastor's dark deeds. Souls were delivered because of his work. Realms became more powerful.

*The light engulfed Alastor, searing through his ethereal form
with a cleansing fervor.
With a deafening roar that echoed through the night, the
Demon dissipated, his form unraveling into fading wisps of
darkness that dispersed into the ether.*

THOSE WISPS of darkness dispersed into the ether, only to collect in their rightful place. Hell. Alastor's threads of darkness collected in a tornado of dark vapors, whirring and spiraling as all the molecules and energy combined and reformed him. A Demon such as Alastor only died by fire.

-The End-

PREVIEW OF SHADOWS OF DESTINY (VEIL OF SHADOWS 9) [UNEDITED]

ABOUT SHADOWS OF DESTINY

In a world where Angels plot and Demons scheme, Jed and Shay must fight for survival at every turn.

If looks could kill, Alastor would raze all of Hell in retribution. He didn't appreciate being sent home in a blast of light with everything he'd built destroyed, and he's going to do everything in his power to hunt down the half-breed who did it.

For Jed and Shay, Hell is filled with challenges, from hiding a stolen Angel baby to being a body double for the Queen; these two have their work cut out for them.

Now, if only Jed could get over his guilt for tearing Shay away from her normal life.

Note to readers:

This book is a bridge between Veil of Shadows 5 & 6 and Jed and Shay's timeline. It brings both stories up to date and readies them for future books. This book contains chapters from Veil of Shadows: Nightjar. I couldn't write about Jed and Shay's time in Hell and skip over those scenes, they were too important in Jed and Shay's growth. Some have been expanded on and written more in depth for Jed and Shay's story. Enjoy, I'm happy you are here.

Chapter 1

Shay had read enough books from her parent's library to know how to care for a baby. However, none of those books ever touched on the subject of caring for a baby Angel.

Jed was frantically drawing runes, casting protection charms, lining doorways with salt and ash. Sweat dripped down his face as he worked. He took off his shirt and wipe it away.

For the first time, Shay noticed the runes tattooed on Jed's skin glowed slightly as he worked.

The baby in her arms squirmed. Shay looked down at the dark haired child in her arms. Large blue eyes searched her face.

Shay smiled. The baby simply stared.

There was blood on the blanket and small drops on the baby's head. Shay licked her finger and wiped them off. She folded the bloody parts of the blanket away from the baby's face and checked him over for injuries. She lifted the folds of baby fat around his neck and arms but found nothing concerning.

The baby yawned and made quiet mewling sounds before his eyes fluttered closed and he fell asleep. Shay rocked the baby and watched Jed as he laid a line of salt across the balcony doors.

There was a thud outside the room. Something pounded on the door.

Jed crossed the room carefully so as not to disturb his hard work.

The pounding became louder.

"Who is it?" Jed asked.

"Let me in," a familiar voice said.

"Not until you tell me who you are."

Shay's eyes were wide as she looked between the sleeping baby in her arms and the door.

Jed was right to be wary of the shit fest Meg had dropped into their arms. Memories of the battles with Angels and Demons flooded Shay. She couldn't imagine fighting like that with a baby to protect.

Chapter 2

Nero galloped across the wasteland of midwestern Hell. Inky seepage dripped down his flank and leg, leaving a hoof-print in the hard packed dirt.

He hadn't felt a thing through the tether to Shay in days. She was here and quiet. Nero had slowed his pace, the wound on his flank throbbing and aching. He surveyed the land ahead, searching for a cool pond to soak in. The ochre sun of Hell wasn't terribly warm, but it still exhausted the stallion. Nero didn't have a good feeling about the wound on his backside. The Crossroads Demon had clawed him back at the ranch and while the wound had festered slowly, it never felt as bad as it did now.

Nero thought about lying down to rest, but he was afraid he wouldn't get up again. Creatures he'd never seen before slithered in the shadowed forests of Hell. The dead walked here as well. The creatures kept their distance. He assumed it was because of the injury or the golden ring in his ear and around his neck. He was more than simply a stallion on the loose in Hell. He had rank. Something he never experienced on the Earthen plane. While Shay cared for him like he was her child, he still lived behind gates and fences. Freedom was new and while Nero enjoyed experimenting with his newly found free will, he missed the days at the ranch with Shay.

He'd slowed to a snail's pace without realizing it. Nero hung his head, afraid he'd never make it to Shay in time.

There was a sudden tugging along the tether that joined

him to Shay. Nero's eyes went wide as he realized she was afraid. Whatever was going on, she still wasn't safe.

Nero dug deep down. He whinnied and shook his head, gathering strength he didn't think he had, then picked up his pace to a gallop again.

Continue the series with Shadows of Destiny

About the Author

M. R. Pritchard writes about the elemental struggle between good and evil, and gods and monsters, and about people who turn into gods and monsters. Usually with a mix of apocalypse or post-apocalyptic setting. She also includes a spec of a love story because what is humanity without love?

M. R. Pritchard is a two-time Kindle Scout winning author, her short story "Glitch" has been featured in the 2017 winter edition of THE FIRST LINE literary journal. Her short story "Moon Lord" has been featured in Chronicle Worlds: Half Way Home (Part of the Future Chronicles) and will be time capsuled on the moon on the Lunar Codex in 2024. M. R. Pritchard holds degrees in Biochemistry and Nursing. She is a northern New Yorker transplanted to the Gulf Coast of Florida who enjoys coffee, mint chocolate, cloudy days, and reading on the lanai.

Visit her website MRPritchard.com and Subscribe. You'll get subscriber only content, updates, special previews of new projects, and book deals.

ALSO BY M. R. PRITCHARD

Other Books by M. R. Pritchard

Science Fiction/post-apocalyptic:

The Phoenix Project

The Reformation

Revelation

Inception

Origins

Resurrection

The Phoenix Project Compendium Edition

The Safest City on Earth

The Man Who Fell to Earth

Heartbeat

Asteroid Riders Series

Moon Lord

Collector of Space Junk and Rebellious Dreams

Steampunk:

Tick of a Clockwork Heart

Dark Fantasy:

Sparrow Man Series/Veil of Shadows Series

Sparrow Man

Nightingale Girl

Scarecrow

Raven King

Nightjar

Night Owl

Etched in Darkness

Embrace the Night

Shadows of Destiny (forthcoming)

Midnight Serenade (forthcoming)

Thread the Bone

Fantasy/Fairy Tale Love Story/Romance:

Muse

Forgotten Princess Duology

Midsummer Night's Dream: A Game of Thrones

Poetry/Short Stories

Consequence of Gravity

www.ingramcontent.com/pod-product-compliance
Lightning Source LLC
Chambersburg PA
CBHW061819190726
48289CB00007B/2252